Megalomaniac

By Jack Bell

Order this book online at www.trafford.com
or email orders@trafford.com

Most Trafford titles are also available at major online book retailers.

Print information available on the last page.

ISBN: 978-1-4907-8236-2 (sc)
ISBN: 978-1-4907-8238-6 (hc)
ISBN: 978-1-4907-8237-9 (e)

Library of Congress Control Number: 2017910629

Trafford rev.   07/19/2017

Trafford
PUBLISHING®   www.trafford.com
North America & international
toll-free: 1 888 232 4444 (USA & Canada)
fax: 812 355 4082

meg·a·lo·ma·ni·a

/megələˈmānēə/

noun

A delusional mental illness that is marked by feelings that you are much more important, wealthy, and powerful than you really are. A person with this manic or paranoid disorder is referred to as a "Megalomaniac".

I would like to thank you all for donating to my GoFundMe campaign and helping me get the book published.

Kim Spencer, Danny Mancha, Tom Gunther, Larry Littrell, John Bell, Eric Wright, Bob Kimpton, Irene Vazquez, Krissi Clowers, Harry Seaward, Mark and Angie Lowman, Ronny Reynoso, Bridget Mata, Rachel Butler, Ken Day, Tori White, Tracy Decker, Mike and Shawna Babbitt, Chris Coakley, Mike Morgan, Jolie Brown, Jesse Adams, David Cartwright, George Reynoso, Teddy Boykin, Jason Becker, Dave James, Todd Taylor, Deborah Winslow, Jennifer Spurlock, Racey Mullins, Cory Mitchell, Joe Poznoski, Thomas Garner, Valarie Hunt, Reuben Patton, Karen MacPhee, Jack Grisham, Donna Moges, Kathy Shanley, Kristine Hansen, John O'Neill, Stacy Yard, Robert Faiella, Jennifer Alogna, Don Brower, Brad Tinsman, Sherice Davis, and Anthony and Stacey Balboa.

I would also like to thank: Anthony Balboa, Bobby Rio, George Reynoso, Zachary Torres, and Darcy Lucero for the photographs they took of me for this book.

Special thanks to:
Robert Butler for the front and back cover artwork.
Anthony Balboa for the title page picture.
Patrick George for his drawing for the story "Social Media Junkie".
Zachary Torres for the back cover photograph.
And
Jack Grisham for the back cover authors portrait.

Contents

My Secret Place

I grew up in Garden Grove, California. My parents own a house that has a three-fourth-acre backyard. One of the biggest properties in the city. Along the south border of the yard is what my friends and I used to refer to as "the Ditch." My parents called it a canal, but the proper term for it is a flood control channel. This flood control channel ran for miles east into Long Beach and west into Santa Ana. I used it as a kind of highway to get to places like school and friends' houses. I could walk or even ride my motocross bike freely in the ditch without having to deal with people. An occasional rat or possum didn't care if I smoked pot or a cigarette. I could sit in the shade under the streets and drink a beer down there, and nobody said shit! Under each street and intersection are drainage tunnels. Some are big enough to bend down and walk through, and some are small where you would have to crawl on your belly like a lizard to get to the top. At the end of each tunnel is a cement room with a manhole in the ceiling that goes up to the sidewalk. From the street, you would see these as long rectangular spaces in the curb with metal bars going across them so large pieces of trash can't wash into them when it rains and people are kept out. Usually they are at intersections and under bus stops. These were my secret places. I only took high-ranking friends and family into those rooms. Security clearance was necessary to keep my places secret. Whenever I took someone to a cement room, I only took them back to that same room. I never showed them a different one. I explored every tunnel and room within miles of my house. I knew the sewers like the back of my hand. I wasn't a hoodlum; I was a hood rat! I lost the police down there many times. I used to ditch school a lot. The cops and truant officers would chase me during school hours trying to impose their will upon me. I would just jump in the ditch and scurry into the nearest tunnel to escape. I would navigate my way through the sewer and pop up through a manhole, like a gopher, hundreds of feet behind them. Sometimes, I would light up a cigarette, hide in the bushes, and watch them as they looked for me. They would rip their shirts on the fence and then try to slide down the twenty-foot cement wall without falling on their faces. All the while thinking they had me trapped down there. It was hilarious! They thought they had me cornered. Sometimes, the fat ones would get stuck down there, and a firetruck would have to come and drop a rope so they could climb out. This was better than watching TV to me. Better than playing a video game. I had my own private *Keystone Cops* comedy show every time they chased me. I knew if they ever caught me, even though I was a kid, they would beat the shit out of me, but I was never apprehended. Oh, and at night after a backyard party or street fight, forget about it. I was like a ghost. POOF! Gone. The truant officer at my high school was named was Mr. Janakowski. When I did go to school, which wasn't very often, and I would see him and would always give him a wink. He used to say, "If I ever catch you off this property, you little shit . . ." shaking his fist at me. He's most likely dead now, but he probably thought about me long after I got kicked out of that school.

Behind my house is a large intersection, and on the other side of the street is a park. On the corner is a bus stop with a bench, and behind that are basketball courts. Underneath the bus stop is one of my secret places. It was a Saturday, and I was a little bored, so I jumped into the ditch and went to that secret place to smoke a cigarette. While I was down there, I could hear the people above me talking. They were sitting on the bus stop bench and had no idea I was below them. I could also hear the guys playing basketball behind them. From my point of view, I could only see the bottom of the cars and their tires as they made right turns at the intersection and went north. Then the idea hit me. Bing! Like a lightbulb above my head. I scurried down the hole and into the ditch, up the wall, and over the fence, and within minutes, I was in my house. I had just gotten a brand-new "wrist rocket." A wrist rocket is a fancy metal slingshot that wraps around your wrist for stability as you grip the front of it with the fist of your left hand. It has long rubber tubes that you stretch back and a leather pouch that you can put a rock or whatever you want to shoot into it. So you just pinch the pouch with your right thumb and index finger, pull it back, aim, and shoot. People actually use these things for hunting animals in the woods, and for competitions, but here in the city, all I had were the stupid bullseye targets that came with it in the box. I was ready to put it to good use.

Luckily, my parents weren't home. I went into their room and got my dad's binoculars out of the closet. I had to do some surveillance on my victims. I went out to the back fence and climbed up to take a look. There were two people on the bench and about five or six guys in the basketball court. Perfect. There was also a driveway to enter the parking lot just past the bus stop. Earlier that week, I was ditching school at the railroad tracks behind my house, and I found an old Pachinko machine that someone had dumped there. It was all broken up and the glass was cracked, but the balls were still in it. I took a rock and broke all the glass out and collected the balls. They were a little smaller than a marble, but they were made of metal, not glass. Perfect ammo for my wrist rocket. Leaving the binoculars leaning on the fence, I went back to the house and retrieved my weapon. I put the balls in a ziplock bag, and I was ready. My plan was to see if I could get the people at the park into a fight with a passing car. If I shot the side of a turning car with a Pachinko ball, maybe they would get mad and pull into the parking lot. I hid down in my secret place like Gollum in the darkness with my precious wrist rocket in hand. I waited for the light to turn green. I pulled back my sling. I let the first car go by, lucky bastards, but I nailed the second car right on the bottom

3

of the door. They didn't stop. I let another car pass. I would choose who got it and who didn't in this game. I was the lord of the underworld. I hit another car. Still nothing. I started to think that my plan wasn't going to work. Like I said, I was bored, and I wanted some action! Then I heard it. The car waiting at the light was playing loud music. When the light turned green, just as he was turning, I pulled back and shot it right off the middle of their door panel. They screeched to a halt right in front of me. I could tell that it was a nice car because the rims were chrome and shiny.

A guy rolled down the window and said to the people on the bench, "Did you just throw a fucking rock at our car?"

I scurried down the tunnel and ran as fast as I could back into my yard. I grabbed the binoculars. The car I hit was a low rider with four Mexican men inside. I was so excited I could barely hold the binoculars still so I could look through them. They had pulled into the parking lot and parked. The two guys sitting in the front of the car had gotten out and were yelling at the two people on the bench. My plan worked! It was actually fucking happening!

Unfortunately, there were two things that were wrong. Number one was that I couldn't hear what they were saying to each other because I was too far away. Number two was that the people on the bench were a woman and a boy, so I didn't think the gang members were going to fight with them. I thought to myself that this was my first try, and I would have to work out some kinks. What I didn't expect happened next. With all the commotion going on at the bus stop bench, I had forgotten about the guys playing basketball. They were all black men, and when they saw what was happening, they stopped playing and walked over to the fence. I can't tell you exactly what was said because I was just reading their body language. They must have told the Mexicans to leave the people on the bench alone. Then they started pointing fingers at each other.

Holy shit, I thought. *What is happening?*

The two other Mexican guys got out of the car, and the black guys came around the fence. They started yelling at each other. I saw the driver point to his vehicle. My plan was working! This was better than any TV show or video game. This was live action, and I created it! The biggest black guy and the biggest Mexican started pushing each other. They did this a few times and then it was on! They were full-on fighting. Circling each other, they started out boxing. Then after a minute or two, they took it to the ground. The black guy was getting the better of the Mexican on the ground, so he stood back up, but he was getting beat up standing too. All of a sudden, one of the other Mexican guys pulled out a gun and shot It In the air.

Oh no, that's not good, I thought.

The people at the bus stop hid behind the bench. The black guys backed off. The Mexicans all got back in their car, did a burnout, and got out of there.

After a minute, the bus came and picked up the woman and the boy and took them to wherever they were going. The black guys went back on the other side of the fence and started playing basketball again. And with a blink of an eye, everything was back to normal. The cops didn't even come.

"Wow! That was awesome," I said out loud.

It was my game, and I was the puppet master. I pulled the strings! None of those people had an inkling of a clue that a twelve-year-old kid had just made them do what they did. Made that happen within their lives. Then watched it unfold with his father's binoculars from afar. They each had a story to tell their friends and family when they got home, but to this day, they didn't know it was premeditated, planned in advance by a boy who was bored.

Just then, my mother called me from the house, "Hey, what are you doing out there?"

"Oh, nothing. I'm just bird watching with Dad's binoculars," I yelled back.

"Well, we brought back lunch for you and your brother, so come in and eat."

That's great! I thought.

I was hungry. In all that excitement and running back and forth, I had worked up an appetite. I climbed down from the fence and started walking toward the house. I remember hoping they had brought us some McDonald's.

I did this every weekend for about a month or maybe two. I documented the people on the bench and at the basketball court like an oceanographer would tag a shark. I did this so I would never get caught, and I never was. Playing the game with the same people twice might give me and my secret place away. This was unacceptable. I eventually shot my brother with the wrist rocket, and my parents took it away from me. That is when the game ended. I still went down to my secret place but never shot at another car. The last person I took down there was my daughter. I wanted her to see where I used to spend my personal time. She was a teenager when I showed her my secret place. Around the same age as I was when I dwelt there. Now I am too old to go down there. I would probably get stuck like the cops did when I was younger. I will tell you this, though. I still remember where every tunnel goes, every crack and crevice in the sewer system, and where every manhole comes up to the street or sidewalk. So if I really needed to go down there, you would never catch me.

Possession?

I was sitting on my porch smoking a cigarette. It was a bright sunny Sunday morning, and I was a little slow from drinking too much the night before. It was summertime, and I liked sitting there watching the girls in their bikinis ride by on their beach cruisers and my neighbors stumbling out of their apartments feeling as bad or worse than I did. The sun felt good on my face as I tried to recall the events of the previous evening. Nope. Nothing. I must have blacked out. I remember going to the bar with a friend in the early evening, meeting some girls, and doing shots with them. Drinking with my friend and some of the patrons I knew there. But as to how I got home or in my apartment, I have no clue. There was no sign that one of the girls had come home with me either, so how did I get there? I was dreading doing the walk of shame around my block searching for a clue as to where I parked my truck, as I had done so many times before. That's when she walked up to me. She had stringy blond hair with black roots showing at the top. VERY skinny. She was wearing a black tank top, black pants, and black boots, which wasn't what I found strange. There were a lot of goth girls in the downtown Huntington Beach area. What I did find strange was not just one thing, but two. First were her tattoos. I have tattoos, and just about everyone I know has them, but her tattoos were unlike any I had ever seen before. Some kind of Egyptian hieroglyphs or Satanic symbols. Definitely not done by anyone I knew around here. Second was the dog she was walking. A HUGE Doberman pinscher. Probably weighed more than she did.

"Hello," she said in a German accent, I think.

"Hi," I said.

"Do you have an animal in your apartment?"

"Excuse me?"

"An animal. Do you have any animals in your apartment?"

At this point, I was very confused because I didn't have any pets at all. Not even a goldfish.

"No, I don't have any animals. Why do you ask?" I said.

"I was walking by your apartment last night, and your door was wide open. All the lights were off and it was very dark inside."

"Okay."

"Well, my Bruno began to bark at the open door, which is unusual, because he is usually very tame."

I looked at the dog, and he was just staring at me. I noticed that his stubbed tail wasn't wagging.

"And?" I said.

"He seemed to want to attack something in your living room, but it was too dark in there to see what it was."

"Are you sure it was *this* apartment?" I asked.

"Oh, yes. I am positive it was this apartment," she said confidently.

"Where do you live?"

"Just down the road." She pointed south down Huntington Street toward the beach.

Now I had been living in that apartment for eight years and knew all the neighbors. I had never in my life seen this woman before. I think I would have remembered a tatted-down goth chick with a German accent and a huge Doberman!

"So what did you do?"

"Well, it took all of my might to hold him back from running into your living room. He is much stronger than me, you know. Then from out of the darkness I heard a strange growl, like that of an animal. It started out very faint, but then grew louder and louder. Bruno stopped barking and began to whine as if he was in fear. The growling did not sound like a human, so then I was afraid as well. That is why I asked you if you had an animal in there."

"Well, I don't. Come look for yourself."

She reluctantly walked toward my front door and peered inside.

"Come on in," I said, but she would not enter.

"No, that's okay. I believe you," she said.

"But there was definitely something in there last night. I'm sure of it!"

"Well, I was home last night, and I can assure you there were no animals in my apartment."

"Okay, if you say so."

We both stood there for a moment not really sure what to say to each other. I walked over to Bruno and petted him on the head.

"See, he's not afraid of me," I said.

"Okay then, have a nice day," she said tugging on Bruno's leash.

I watched her walk north on Huntington, make a right on Nashville, and then she was gone. I scratched my head, trying to comprehend the conversation I had just had with her. I walked into my kitchen, got a beer out of the fridge, and popped it open. I tried again to remember what had happened the night before. Nothing. Was there an animal in my apartment last night? Maybe something got in here when I was at the bar and left before I got home. There were no signs of hair or paw prints or anything like that. Had I gone temporarily mad in a drunken blackout and growled at Bruno from the darkness? If so, what the hell was I doing sitting in my living room, in the dark, in the middle of the night, with my door wide open? Did I turn into a fucking werewolf? No, I thought, my clothes weren't ripped up. I remembered in the movies whenever a guy turns into a werewolf, for some reason his clothes always get ripped up. Maybe she was a ghost and she was never even there? Did I imagine her? No, I actually touched the dog when I petted it. She might have been a witch, testing me with one of her spells. After all, I had never seen her before, and after that day, I never saw her again! Plus, she had all those weird tattoos from God knows where. Maybe I was possessed by a demon of hers or something. I remembered in the movie *The Exorcist* how Linda Blair's character growled like an animal. I laughed to myself and walked back to my front door. Two girls in bikinis rode by on their beach cruisers. I took a swig from my beer. What *had* happened last night? Neither I nor the world will ever know.

Matsu's Feng Shui

My friends Tyler and Ilene had planned a birthday party for Ilene at Matsu Japanese Restaurant in Huntington Beach, California. I was at home with my girlfriend Sheena waiting for her to get ready, as usual. She had very long beautiful curly hair, but it would take her an hour to straighten it with her curling iron, or whatever the thing is that she used. Now here's the catch. I was the one who liked her hair straight, but I had no patience to wait for her to do it. So I would sit in the living room, drink beer, and yell things at her to make her hurry up, which in turn would put her in a shitty mood.

"Let's go already. We're gonna be late!" I yelled at the bathroom where she was.

No answer.

"Just leave it curly. It looks fine."

Again, no answer.

"Don't make me come in there and sing the song!"

"I'll be out in a minute. Have another beer," she yelled back.

I went to the fridge and got another beer.

"If you're not done by the time I finish this beer I'm gonna start singing the song!"

"You better not, Jack. I'm doing this for you! I'm almost done."

I downed the beer in two big gulps and ran over to the bathroom. I started singing the Ramones song:

"Sheena is a punk rocker, Sheeeena is a punk rocker, Sheena is a punk rocker, Now-oh-now!"

I would stand at the door of the bathroom and repeat these lyrics over and over and over and over again until she finished. She hated this because she didn't like punk rock music, so it made her finish faster, at least in my mind.

By the time she got done, I had already drunk six beers and two shots of Jamison Irish Whiskey, so I was pretty buzzed. We got Ilene's present, got into Sheena's car 'cause I couldn't drive, and headed to Matsu. Here's the funny part: after all that, we were the first ones there! I told Sheena I'd make it up to her by buying her a drink at the bar. We got a small table. I walked up to the bar alone and ordered a glass of wine for her and a beer and a shot of whiskey for me. I did the shot real quick and gave the shot glass back to the bartender giving him a wink. I took the wine and the beer back to the table.

"Did you do a shot when you were at the bar?" she said.

"No," I said in my best surprised face.

"Why, do you want one?"

"No. You better pace yourself, Jack. We have a long night ahead of us."

As usual, she was right. It was Saturday afternoon, and the sun was still up. I was feelin' good!

Pie and Trixie were next to arrive, and I could tell by the look on Trixie's face that Pie was in no better shape than I was. We greeted each other, and I suggested that Pie and I should go get the girls drinks at the bar. We went to the bar and ordered two more beers, two more wines, and I ordered two more shots. Pie and I did the shots real quick, but this time, the bartender winked at us. This was going to be a good night! We went back to the table and brought the girls their drinks. I could tell that they had already been talking about us being drunk when we were at the bar. Mack and Kellie-Kelly got there next, and we did the same thing with Mack, three more shots. Then Chewy got there, and we did it with Chewy, four shots. Tyler and Ilene are ALWAYS the last ones to arrive, even to their own party. By this time, I had drunk four beers and four shots of whiskey, plus the six beers and two shots at home, for a grand total of ten beers and six shots. Pie was right there with me. We all went into the backroom and got seated at this long table. We ordered more drinks and then food. We had all known each other since high school and were like a big happy drunk family, which is nice, but Pie and I were always the worst and would usually end up either yelling and cursing at each other by the end of the night or hugging and kissing each other like a couple of homos. That night we were homos, so Sheena and Trixie could breathe easy. We all talked and drank and ate our dinners. Everyone was having a great time. I noticed that Pie's eyes were looking heavy, and he was starting to fall asleep. Sometimes, when he did this, his face would go right into his plate of food, which to me is hilarious, not so much to Trixie.

"Let's do presents!" I yelled, which woke Pie up a little.

"I love you. You have beautiful feet," Pie said to Ilene.

"I'm gonna order that volcano drink!" Chewy said with a big smile.

"I am too!" I said.

"No, you're not! No more hard alcohol for you," Sheena said, and I'm glad she did.

Sheena was of Irish and Russian decent. What a mix! She was a good caring girlfriend to me when she wasn't drunk and could fuck like a racehorse. The only bad thing was when we were drunk together, we fought like cats and dogs. I was drunk most of the time, and we both had BAD tempers, so we didn't last long.

Chewy ordered the volcano drink, and Ilene opened her presents while Trixie kept Pie's head out of his plate of food. We were all pretty buzzed, especially the guys. Tyler and Mack were catching up to me and Pie fast, because we were running out of steam, when they brought Chewy his volcano drink. The drink (I can't remember the actual name) was a big martini glass with lots of different hard alcohol mixed to make it look red and a floater of 151 Bacardi on top, which they lit on fire before they served it to you. I am SOOOOO glad Sheena didn't let me order that drink! They put it in front of Chewy.

"How the fuck you gonna drink that?" Tyler said laughing.

"You're gonna burn your eyebrows off," Mack added with a big smile.

"Don't be a pussy! Drink it!" I yelled across the table.

Pie just nodded his head. Sheena, Trixie, Kellie-Kelly, and Ilene just sat there waiting for it to happen.

"Drink it, Chewy! Drink It!" I yelled again. After all, my nickname for our group is Super-Asshole!

I don't know what Chewy was thinking, and to his credit, I probably wouldn't have done much better. He put the glass up to his mouth to drink it without blowing out the flame first, so he singed his goatee, eyebrows, and hair all at once. Then, in a fit of panic from being burned, he threw the glass down on the table. The tablecloth caught on fire, and his whole fucking end of the table went up in flames! Now I was at the head of the table on one side, and Chewy was at the head of the other. Everybody else was sitting on the sides. I thought that this was the funniest thing I'd ever seen! Not thinking of course that the whole restaurant could go up in flames, and since we were in the back, we could all die. Everyone backed away from the table except for Pie, who just sat there not really realizing what was going on, and me. I was laughing so hard I think I may have pissed my pants a little. Tyler, Mack, and Kellie-Kelly got their water glasses and threw them on the fire putting it out. EVERYONE in the restaurant was just looking at us. Just picture this scene. Smoke is billowing in the air from the burnt tablecloth. Water is now all over our table, so everything on that side is wet. Chewy is standing at one end of the table with all the hair on his face and head singed. Everyone else is just standing there at the side of the table in the smoke. Pie is still trying to figure out what just happened, and I'm sitting there drunk laughing my ass off! Now our bill on a normal night for the nine of us is usually $700 to $900. Most of that alcohol. This night was gonna be a little more! Needless to say, they NEVER served that drink at Matsu again. To this day, if you even mention it, they give you a dirty look! Chewy was all right; he didn't really get burned, just minus some facial hair. Sheena, Trixie, Kellie-Kelly, and Ilene did a good job of getting us toward the front door. I was very drunk, and my balance was way off. As you exit the restaurant off to the right side, there is a koi fish pond with a water fountain made of bamboo in the middle of it. As I walked by the fountain, you can probably guess what happened. Yes, I fell in the pond. I was just walking by the pond, minding my own business, and some kind of vortex fucking vacuum sucked me right into the goddamn thing. The next thing I remember is I am splashing around in the pond in my nicest clothes; by the way, the fountain is smashed to pieces, and koi fish are swimming all around my ass! Now Pie is laughing his ass off at me, and Sheena is trying to help me out of it. I am so drunk that I keep slipping and now Sheena is getting all wet. Finally, one of the guys, I don't remember who, helped me out of the pond. I am soaking wet. We finally make it out of the place and everyone is cracking up! Except Sheena of course because she was so embarrassed. Pie can barely stand now because he is laughing so hard.

"You fucked up the feng shui!" Pie yelled.

"You fucked up Matsu's feng shui! We're gonna come back here next week, and this place is gonna be a fuckin' Mexican food restaurant!" He was still laughing hysterically and could barely talk.

Pie fell to his knees. Then everyone started laughing, even Sheena! I was laughing at Pie who was laughing at me. We were all just standing in the parking lot laughing at each other. Me soaking wet, Chewy with burnt hair, and Pie on his knees. It was a great fucking night!

I did go back there about a week later. I went by myself, without Sheena, and no, it wasn't a Mexican food restaurant. It was still Matsu. I walked in the front door and looked at the pond. There was yellow "Caution" tape all around the front of it. The fountain was still all broken up, and there was a little sign sticking out of it that said "Under Construction." I had to hold back from laughing. I walked to the back and they had a new tablecloth on the table, and everything seemed fine. Walking back toward the bar, I made eye contact with the bartender. It was the same guy from the week before, but he didn't wink at me this time; he gave me a look like "You should be ashamed of yourself." I guess the feng shui was all right, and Matsu survived Ilene's birthday party. What they didn't know was that my birthday was coming up next.

Candi's Not a Stranger

It was about 10:00 a.m. on a Tuesday when my phone got a text message. I was still in bed and reached over to see who could be bothering me at this ungodly hour. It was my friend Candi. The text simply said, "Around?" Now I know this is only one word, but I knew exactly what it meant. She wanted me to go buy some beer, come over her house, and have sex with her. One little word said all that. So I responded, "I am now. What's up?" Her response was, "Wanna play?" Now I had just woken up and had a rock-hard boner, so I thought what the hell. I responded, "What about your sugar daddy?" Candi: "Don't worry about him. He won't be home till 5:00 p.m. We have plenty of time." Me: "I'll be over in a bit." That was all that was said.

Now here's the thing about Candi. I have known her for about fifteen years, and we would hook up here and there, off and on. She is a very pretty blond-haired, blue-eyed nymphomaniac with an amazing body. At this time, though, she was living with this older rich biker guy whom she called her "sugar daddy" in a big five-bedroom house. During the day when he was at work, she would get lonely and bored because even though he paid for everything, he was older and didn't take care of her in the sack. So she would just drink beer, watch TV, play with herself, and fuck around on Facebook all day till he got home. I got out of bed and jumped in the shower, got dressed, and walked out the door. It was January, but it was warm and sunny out like summertime. I had on a T-shirt, board shorts, and flip-flops. I thought to myself, *This is going to be a great day! What could go wrong?* I got in my truck, and when I started it up, the song "Hotel California" by Eagles was on the radio. The morning sun felt good, and I backed out of the driveway. I stopped at Wal-Mart and grabbed a shopping cart. I went to the beer aisle and put a twelve-pack in it. Then I thought I'd better get some condoms because there's no way in hell that I want to knock this crazy bitch up! I walked over to the pharmacy and got a box of condoms. I also needed smokes, but at Wal-Mart, you can't get them in a checkout line, so you have to go to the side of the store where the manager is. I looked down at my cart and saw all I had was beer and condoms. It was 11:00 a.m., and there wasn't that many people in the store. I pondered buying some food or a pack of gum or something, but then I just thought, fuck it. I walked up to the manager's counter and put up the beer.

"I'll need a pack of Marlboros too," I said.

She turned and got the smokes and rang up the beer and the cigarettes.

"Oh and these too."

I threw the condoms on the counter. After she rang up the rubbers, she looked up at me with a hint of disgust. Here it was eleven in the morning, and I'm buying beer, cigarettes, and condoms.

"I'm having a party," I said feeling a little bit ashamed.

"I'll bet you are," she said judgmentally.

I just smiled a big smile and looked at her boobs.

"You want to come?"

"Maybe another time." She cracked a tiny smile.

I winked at her as I turned and walked away feeling triumphant.

I got to Candi's front gate, but the code she gave me wasn't working. I tried it again and again, but it didn't work. I thought, *Shit after all that, I can't get in!* Then some old lady on the other side left, so I snuck in through the outdoor. I parked a little ways away from her place; after all, this wasn't my first rodeo, and I needed an escape plan in case the shit hit the fan. I walked up to her door. Of course, it was open, so I walked inside. Her bedroom was at the top of this big staircase, so I called, "Ahoy."

"Come on up," she called back.

I walked up the stairs, and she was laying on her bed looking at her phone.

"Put that thing away right now, young lady, or I'm gonna have to spank you!"

She just looked up and smiled.

"You know you shouldn't leave your front door open like that. Anyone could just come in here and rape you."

"That's what I was hoping for," she replied.

"Well, your knight in shining armor is here with beer!"

"My hero."

"Well, I wouldn't go that far, my lady."

"Enough with the pleasantries, so you wanna fuck?"

She just smiled again and said, "Gimme a beer first, punk ass."

I sat on her bed and popped two beers. I put the cable box on a classic rock music station, and lo and behold, "Hotel California" was on again. I thought, well, that's a coincidence. She was a good conversationalist, and we talked about some old friends we had in common and what they were doing now. How our daughters were doing. About how nice the weather was for January. Blah, blah, blah. Then she started telling me about how her and her sugar daddy had gone to a club a few weeks past. She met some guy she liked and started giving him a blow job under the table. Now I thought that was a little weird, but what the hell, she wasn't my girlfriend, so who am I to judge? Anyway, her sugar daddy came back from the bathroom and caught them in the act. Well, I guess he got all bent out of shape—who could blame him?—and they left the bar. I laughed and told her what a slut she was, and she laughed too. Then a thought came into my head.

"How about we do a reenactment?" I said half-joking, half-not.

"What?"

"How about a blow job?"

She looked at me with a smirk like "Okay, you asshole" and then, without saying a word, pulled down my shorts and put her head down. We had sex for a while and then finished up. I popped a few more beers and sat back on the bed. By this time, it was about 2:00 p.m. We sat and talked some more and listened to music on the cable station. She mentioned that she had found some pictures of us and a bunch of our friends from the old days. I said, "That's cool, let's check them out." So she went and got them I started going through them. We reminisced awhile, and she gave me a few photos that had me and her together in them.

"I'm horny again," she said with a nasty look on her face.

"What?"

"I want you to fuck me again."

I looked at the clock, and it was after 3:00 p.m.

"I had better get going. Your sugar daddy will be home soon," I said knowing I shouldn't.

"Just one more time before you go. I promise I'll make it worth your while!"

"Okay, geez. Just let me finish my beer first."

We sat there about another minute. I was almost done with my beer when all of a sudden, the door to her room flew open.

"What the fuck is going on here?" he said with a wild look in his eyes.

It was her sugar daddy. He had come home from work early. A minute later and he would have caught us in the act going for round number two! Thoughts raced through my mind. He was blocking the door, and I was on the second floor, no escape. Shit! I instantly put my calm, no-big-deal face on. Years of training in MMA taught me that in this situation, defend, don't provoke. This asshole could have a gun or a knife. If he didn't, I could take him easily, but I didn't want it to come down to that.

"You fucking whore! Can't I leave you alone for one second?" he screamed.

"Calm down, Ned. There's nothing going on."

But I could hear a crackling in her voice, and if I could hear it, so could he. I had to say something fast!

"Ya man, there's nothing going on here. We're just old friends looking at some pictures from when Candi worked at the bar."

I raised a picture of us like an idiot to show him. Thank God there were still a bunch of photographs laying on the bed.

"Look the bed isn't even messed up," I said calmly.

He looked at the bed and then back at me.

"Who the hell are you?"

"He's my friend Jack from Sugars. We're just looking at pictures and drinking beers," she replied.

"Oh, the same Jack that you told me about that can cum five times in one night!"

"One and the same," I said proudly but at the same time trying not to sound like an asshole.

I looked at her like really, you told him that? What the fuck!

"But that was a long time ago, dude. I can't do that anymore." I was lying.

"We're just friends, I swear." I wasn't lying.

"Well, did she tell you about how she blew some asshole at the club the other night right in front of me?"

"Yes, actually she did, and to tell you the truth, brother, I thought that was kind of weird." Again trying not to sound like an asshole, but I just couldn't help it.

She looked at me like really, you just told him that? What the fuck!

He just looked at both of us with a kind of disgusted and confused look on his face. Then there was a moment of brief silence that seemed to last for an eternity. He didn't know what to say. She didn't know what to say. And I just sat there thinking, *All right, what's next?*

He looked at me and said, "You can have her!"

He turned around, slammed the door, and stomped down the stairs. We just sat there and looked at each other.

"Well, that just happened," I said.

She reached down and lit up a cigarette.

"What the hell are you doing?"

"Lighting a cigarette."

"I know you're lighting a cigarette, you crazy bitch. Get your fucking ass down there and make sure he's gone!"

She got up, opened the door, and walked down the stairs. She was gone for a minute and then came back.

"Yeah, he's gone," she said nonchalantly.

I took the cigarette from her hand and took a drag.

"Well, you can stay here now if you want. We're already busted."

"Are you insane? I'm getting the fuck out of here!"

But for a microsecond I did think of staying. If she was that crazy, the sex would be off the hook, but I digress. I put on my flip-flops and got the hell out of that house. When I got to the door, I looked both ways like a little kid crossing the street for the first time. I walked, didn't run, but walked quickly to my truck. Got in and went the opposite direction to throw off anybody trying to tail me and got out the front gate. I know he has a black car, so when I got out to the boulevard, I watched my rear-view mirror, again to make sure I wasn't being followed. When I got back to my neck of the woods, I felt safe. I realized that I had left my damn beer there, so I went back to Wal-Mart. I parked and lit up a cigarette. I just sat there and thought, *Damn that was some crazy-ass shit.* My phone rang. It was Candi.

"Are you okay?" I asked.

"Ya, I'm fine."

"So what's up?"

"I just wanted to know if we're down for the same time tomorrow?"

"You are a goddamn crazy person, aren't you?"

"Yes."

"Well, that's the last time I put my quarter in your slot, girlfriend. Game fuckin' over!"

"You'll be back. My pussy is tighter than shit, and I know what you like, Jack."

I hung up and thought, *Son of a bitch, she's right. I will hit that again.*

I got out of my truck and walked into the store. Went to the beer aisle, again, and walked over to the manager's counter. Just my luck, it was the same chick.

"So how did your party go?" she asked.

"It was a hoot!" I replied.

"Well, next time I'll have to see what this is all about."

"Are you married?" I asked.

"No, but I have a boyfriend," she said.

"Well, let's just say, he's not invited then."

She smiled at me the same way Candi did when I walked up her stairs and into her room a few hours earlier. She slipped me her phone number when I grabbed my beer. As I walked away, I thought, *Here we go again. Fuck!*

Notes from a Speed Freak

A tweaker friend of mine had been up on the drug crystal meth for about three days or so with no sleep at all. He stumbled over to my house for some reason, as many people used to do in those days. It was myself, the tweaker, my brother Steve, and our friend John. You must realize that this was many years before the television show *Breaking Bad*. These are notes that I took of a conversation that we had that afternoon as we sat in my room. This is exactly what was said:

Jack: How do you feel?

Tweaker: Translucid.

Steve: Why do you feel this way?

Tweaker: No more questions today, please.

Steve: Sorry.

Tweaker: Thank you.

John: But why?

Tweaker: I've come to fill my tank.

Jack: Why?

Tweaker: I've come for consultation. (Gives us a middle finger.)

Jack: No, why do you feel translucid?

Tweaker: Hey, this is that "you're mommy's dead" song. (He was referring to the song that was playing on my stereo—"I Saw Your Mommy" by Suicidal Tendencies.)

Steve: (Doesn't say anything but starts laughing uncontrollably.)

John: I think he's totally gone?

Steve: (Just keeps laughing.)

John: Do you know where you're at?

Tweaker: Ozzy's house.

Jack: Are you okay? Can I get you anything?

Tweaker: A beer.

Jack: (I got up and got us all a beer.)

Jack: Feel better?

Tweaker: No.

Steve: So why do you feel translucid?

Tweaker: Because. (Big sigh.)

John: Because you stayed up for two days?

Tweaker: No, because I stayed up for three days.

Jack: Why?

Tweaker: (No response.)

Jack: I'm going to make you a bet.

Tweaker: (Starts to cry.)

Jack: Don't cry, it's all right.

Steve and John: (Start laughing again.)

John: Do you know . . .

Tweaker: (Interrupting John pissed because he was laughing at him crying.) I know that Ozzy is a full-on crazy-looking dude. He's an insane dude and was a cokehead. (He points to a poster of Ozzy that was on my wall.)

John: I was going to say, do you know what day it is?

Tweaker: It's Wednesday. (It was Thursday.)

Tweaker: What's the name of this song?

Steve: (With a big smile on his face.) "Fascist Pig."

Tweaker: Fuck you!

Steve: No, you're not a fascist pig. That's the name of the song. We are still listening to Suicidal Tendencies.

Tweaker: Oh, sorry, wah-ah.

Jack: Don't cry, but I'll bet you that you won't stay awake long enough to finish this conversation. You look pretty tired.

Tweaker: What's your favorite band?

Jack: Black Sabbath.

Steve: Suicidal Tendencies.

John: Misfits.

Tweaker: All those bands suck!

John: Oh ya, well, what's your favorite band?

Tweaker: I don't know.

(There was a lull in the conversation for a minute as we drank our beers, listened to music, and looked at each other.)

Tweaker: I burned a hole in one.

Jack: One what?

Tweaker: Just one.

John: One what? Your nose or your lung?

Tweaker: My lung!

Jack: You were *smoking* crystal meth? Dude, you're crazy?

Tweaker: (Says something unintelligible about his head being in a box and passing out.)

Jack: Well, I won that bet.

Steve: Not really. Now what are you going to do with him, he's passed out?

John: Better hope he doesn't die in here. (Laughing.)

Jack: Shit, I didn't think about that.

I took the beer out from between his legs, walked over to the window, and started pouring it out.

John: Why are you wasting that beer?

Jack: Because that motherfucker probably hasn't brushed his teeth in at least three days. Do you want to drink after him?

Steve: No shit.

John: I guess you're right.

The tweaker was finally sleeping like a baby. Hole in his lung and all.

Steve turned the music up, and I popped open three more beers. It was going to be an interesting evening.

Girl of My Dreams

I had a dream this morning that I was in love with this beautiful, smoking-hot girl. We were at a grocery store kissing, touching, and holding hands. She was putting all her favorite things in the shopping cart and so was I as we walked up and down the aisles together. I could feel the affection I had for her. I wanted to spend the rest of my life with this woman. I was proud and wanted everyone in the store to see me with her. By the way, who are these "dream people"? That is what I call them. I have never seen this girl in my life! There were all these people in the store buying groceries, teenagers picking out magazines at the magazine racks, and checkout ladies at the registers. I have never met or seen any of them before. They're just a bunch of made-up people in my head. None of them ever existed except for a brief moment in a dream. It all seemed so real, though. The love I had for this woman was genuine. Now that I think about it, she literally was the "girl of my dreams." I woke up a little confused. All I could think about after all that was that I didn't even know her name. I just smiled, rolled over, and went back to sleep. Maybe I could find her in another dream and ask her.

On Purpose

I always fuck it up, but what most of them don't realize is that 90% of the time it's on purpose. Maybe it's because they snore or because of the way they laugh. They might tell me that they love me or call me on the phone too much, or maybe not enough. I'll catch them in a lie, or think I do. Want me to meet their friends, or parents, or family, or some other person or people whom they feel are important to them. They'll tell people that I'm an asshole. Or that I drink too much. Or that I'm afraid of commitment knowing it will get back to me. All of which are probably true, but I have seen too many broken marriages, and the guy ALWAYS gets fucked in the end!

Maybe they'll burp, or fart, or sweat too much, or some other gross thing. One of their eyes may not be as straight as the other, or maybe they're too close together, or maybe their nose is too big or too small, or they're too fat or too skinny. Any of a thousand things can set it off.

Don't get me wrong, I love women. That moment when you first meet, your first kiss, your first fuck. You can't wait to see her again, and you get butterflies in your stomach. But then, and it always happens, you have an awkward silence, your first disagreement, your first yelling match, and then it's never the same again. This is when the seed is planted in me and the plan begins to grow. I must get out of this. There are too many women out there to try and fix it. Sit down and talk about our differences or why it's not working out. Go to therapy or get a self-help book, why? For me it's like crawling through broken glass in the slow centuries of hell! You'll never get that "first time you met" feeling back. It is gone forever with that particular person. There are millions of women out there whom I haven't met yet! So then I act like an asshole or get drunk and do or say something mean or stupid, then I'm out, free! Free to go or do whatever I want. Free to meet a new one who has no idea who I am . . . and start again.

Except on nights like tonight when I am lonely and think about all those women in my past and wonder where they are at, what they're doing, and who they are with. Whether they miss or think about me. So that's why I sat down tonight to write this. It's better than calling one of them up and begging for another chance. Pretending to be weak and sorry in hopes of getting laid. So insincere and unoriginal. Foolish.

My phone just rang. It was a girl I met the other day at a gas station. I gave her my number and told her to call me, not taking hers, looking at her straight in the eye trusting that she would call. Confident. Self-assured. Maybe even a little cocky, but not too much. Then a devilish little smile as I walked away and got into my truck and drove away. It worked! I'm meeting her tomorrow for drinks, and she has no idea who I am. And so it starts again . . .

The Grand Olympic Auditorium

When I was a kid back in the 1970s, there was a television show I used to watch called *Lucha Libre*. This was "championship wrestling" and was taped at a place called the Grand Olympic Auditorium in Los Angeles, California. It was on Wednesday nights at 8:30 p.m. on channel 34 and on Saturday nights at 6:00 p.m. on channel 52. I had a small black-and-white television in my room with a wire hanger hanging out the back so I could get better reception on it. My parents wouldn't let me watch it in the living room because they thought it was too violent and bloody. They had no idea that most of it was fake. Now back then, we had dials on the television sets that you had to physically turn with your hand to change the channels. The dial had the numbers 2 through 13 on it representing the different local television stations. In between the 2 and the 13 was something called UHF. This was kind of like cable

TV before there was such a thing. On UHF, you could watch local wrestling and boxing, women's roller derby, horse racing, soap operas in Spanish, and for some reason, shows from England like *Doctor Who* and *Benny Hill*. This is where I would find channels 34 and 52 and watch *Lucha Libre*. The Olympic had the best wrestlers from around the world. People like Gorgeous George, Freddie Blassie, Mil Mascaras, a very young Roddy Piper, and of course Andre the Giant, to name a few. I would just sit in my room and watch these guys beat the shit out of each other. This was very entertaining for an eight-year-old boy. There was also drama in the form of good guys and bad guys, crooked referees, draws where neither guy won, and people getting demasked, except for Mil Mascaras. He NEVER got his mask taken off; I guess that's why his name in English is "Thousand Masks." Then at the end of the show, they would have interviews where the guys would talk smack about each other to promote the next week's broadcast. I even remember the commercial with their phone number, "For tickets call RI 9-5171." The "RI" stood for Richmond, which was the area code for that part of LA before there was area codes. The *R* was number seven on the rotary phone dialer, and the *I* was number four. You may say to yourself, well, that sounds a lot like today's wrestling programs, but it really wasn't. Today, they have huge worldwide pay-per-view extravaganzas that cost millions of dollars to produce. All the main wrestlers have their own action figures and are millionaires. In the '70s, those guys made hardly any money and weren't even on a network television station. They just did it because they loved it. This was happening in my town, and only people who lived in LA or Orange County could watch it on TV or go see it live.

I had just got home from school when I heard a knock at the door. It was my neighbor Picklehead.

"My dad got us four tickets to go see wrestling at the Olympic in LA. Ricky across the street already said that he was in. So you wanna go?"

"Heck yeah I want to go!" I said.

"Well, it's this Saturday, and my dad's going to drive us so be ready to go."

"Okay, I'll be ready," I said excitedly.

You can image how stoked I was to actually be going to see these guys wrestle live! My dad would never take me to an event like this.

Picklehead and I were the same age. He had a kind of elongated skull that was, unless you actually saw him, hard to explain. So all the kids in the neighborhood just called him by that nickname. His family was from Venezuela, and neither one of his parents spoke a word of English. Whenever I would go over his house, he would translate whatever was said between his parents and me. I have no idea how he learned how to write or speak English, but this is how we would communicate when his dad took us on these trips to Los Angeles.

When Saturday came around and it was time to go, I got a few bucks from my mom and ran across the street to Ricky's house. He was a few years older than me, but he was even more into wrestling than I was. Even though he was a white kid, he had some of the masks that the Mexican wrestlers wore, and we would go terrorizing the neighborhood wearing them. I swear I thought that people didn't know who I was when I was wearing one.

"You ready to go, man?" I said.

"Hell yes! This is going to be cool!" Ricky had a big smile.

"Well, let's get over there. We don't want to be late."

When we went over to Picklehead's house, we didn't call him by his nickname because even though his dad didn't speak English, he knew that his son didn't like it, so out of respect, we called him by his real name which was Miguel. His dad had a pickup truck, and only two people could sit in the front, so Ricky and I volunteered to ride in the back. Hell, even if one of us sat in the front, we wouldn't be able to talk to Mr. Miguel anyway. So off we went, an eight-year-old and a twelve-year-old, in the back of a truck with no seat belts. You gotta love it. Going 70 mph up the 5 Freeway with the wind blowing through our hair. We were on our way.

When we got there, I thought the place was gigantic! When you walked down the hallway to the main room, it was draped with huge tapestries of fighters and wrestlers who had fought there in the past. We made our way into the main room and found our seats. It was awesome! The place was filled with gray cigar and cigarette smoke. It smelled like booze, piss, and puke. I thought to myself that my father would NEVER take me to a place like this! I was in heaven.

The first match was some kind of title bout, but Roddy Piper was the referee, so he fucked it all up and caused it to be what they called a "take over" so they would have to do it again. The crowd booed loudly. I booed loudly, threw my fist in the air, and thought, *Fuck you, Roddy Piper!* The next match was a "Mexican Death Match" between, well, you guessed it, two Mexicans. Then the third one was the one I had been waiting for. The champion was Mil Mascaras, and he was going up against the hated Roddy Piper. Piper was doing well at first and got Mascaras in a headlock. He reached over and, to everyone's amazement, pulled off Mil's mask! Of course, he had a mask under his mask, so nobody saw his face, and he pinned Piper and won the match. Seeing Mil Mascaras without his mask back then would have been like seeing KISS without their makeup. That would have been a pretty big deal. Andre the Giant ended the night by winning what was called a "Battle Royal." That's when ten guys get in a ring together, and the last one left wins. All I remember is Andre picking up people over his head and chucking them out of the ring like rag dolls. That was very cool. It was a great night! We went back there a few more times, but that first night was the best. I continued to like wrestling for another year or two. Picklehead's family moved back to Venezuela, and a biker guy moved into their house. When I was about ten years old, I really got into music. Ricky and I got guitars, and that was that. Music would be our love for the rest of our lives. Wrestling was something for little kids and old Mexican men smoking cigars. I'm still friends with Ricky to this day. He is like an older brother to me.

Over the summer, my friend James turned into a punk rocker. I had met him a few years earlier in elementary school, and he was a pretty normal kid. I knew he was a little different because he was adopted, and his parents were kind of old compared to everybody else, but when school started in September, he had changed. He shaved his head and wore boots and a leather jacket. Even when it was hot out, he wore that jacket, so he smelled like body odor. He would come over my house, and my mom didn't like him, which of course made me like him more. He turned me on to all these bands that I didn't even know existed. My older cousins and neighbors had raised me with bands such as Black Sabbath and Led Zeppelin, so it took me a bit to figure out what was going on with these new bands. Some of them didn't even play guitar solos. Hell, a lot of them didn't even know how to play their instruments. One of the bands that I took a liking to was Dead Kennedys. Their lyrics were political, and the guitar player made sounds I had never heard before. I was hooked. Many, many bands came to follow, but Dead Kennedys were my first love.

Later that year, James called me. "Hey, dude, guess who's coming to town!"

"Who?"

"Dead Kennedys, and I got us tickets."

Now I had been to a few concerts at places like the Long Beach Sports Arena, where you sit in your seat and clap properly after each song, but never a punk show.

"Sounds like fun. Where are they playing?" I said nervously.

"Up in LA at a place called the Olympic Auditorium."

"The Olympic Auditorium! I know that place. I've been there before."

"Oh yeah. What bands did you see?" He sounded like I was full of shit.

"I didn't see any bands. I saw championship wrestling matches there when I was a kid."

"Well, this ain't no fake-ass wrestling bullshit. This is a punk rock show!"

"So who all is playing?"

"Well, I already told you Dead Kennedys are headlining, but they're also playing with T.S.O.L., Black Flag, Circle Jerks, Subhumans, and the Dicks."

"Wow, all those bands in one night."

"Yep, it's gonna be awesome!"

"How much is all that gonna cost? Like fifty bucks."

"Try more like $5," he said with a smirk.

"Fuck yeah! I'm in. How are we going to get there? We don't drive or have cars."

"My neighbor Mario has a Volkswagen bus, so we're all gonna pile in there and go together."

"Okay, let's do it!"

The day of the show came, and I was excited and nervous at the same time. I had never felt like that before, after all, now that I think back, I was just a young kid. The concerts I had been to only had an opening band and then the headliner. That was it, just two bands. I had never seen six bands in one night before. I lied to my mom and said I was spending the night at my friend Brian's, but I went straight to James's house. When I got there, they were all drinking beer and smoking pot and cigarettes, so I jumped right in. We were all getting buzzed when James came out with this leather jacket.

"Here, I want you to wear this," he said with a big smile.

"I don't need a jacket. It's hot outside."

"It's not because it's gonna get cold out, dummy. It's so you don't get cut with razor blades when you go in the slam pit."

"Well then, when we get there, I just won't go in."

"Oh believe me, you will want to go in."

I took the jacket but didn't put it on. We all got in the bus. Inside, it had an old sink, but it didn't have running water; it was used as a toilet. We had drunk a lot of beer at the house and had brought a few to the show. If you needed to take a piss, you just stood in front of the sink and pissed down the drain. James was the first to try it out. He stood in front of the sink and started to go. I looked out the back window, and you could see the stream of piss following us down the freeway. I thought that was hilarious! I was the next guy to try it out. I stood in front of the sink carefully aiming my stream into the drain hole. Remember, we were on the freeway going 70 mph. Mario saw me standing there in his rear-view mirror.

"Hey, new kid!" he yelled over the loud stereo.

I turn to my right to see what he wanted. He then swerved the bus over into the left lane causing me to lose my balance and piss all over everyone on that side of the vehicle. The guys tried to get out of the way, but it was too late; my recycled beer was all over them. This was apparently not the first time Mario had done this, so they weren't too mad. Mario was laughing like a hyena.

"Gotcha, motherfucker!" Mario said looking over his right shoulder.

After that, no one attempted to take another piss. Good times, huh? We finally got there and found a spot in the parking lot. We sat outside the bus and started to finish the rest of the beers before we went in. I looked around the parking lot. People were wearing leather jackets and boots. They had mohawks, different-colored hair, makeup on their faces, piercings. I looked down at myself. I was wearing an Ocean Pacific surf shirt, Levi's jeans, and Vans tennis shoes. I decided to put on the leather jacket that James gave me. We finished the beers and started in. The place didn't look as big as I remembered. As we walked in, the tapestries on the walls of the wrestlers looked old and tattered. We walked into the main room, and the first band was already playing. It still smelled the same, like booze and piss, but this time it was mostly clove cigarette and pot smoke in the air. We found a place at the front right of the stage. After the first band finished, the lights came on. I could see that there was a lot more people than when we had first arrived. The place was packed. The second band was Subhumans, and they were apparently from England judging by the singer's accent. When they started, BAM! The place went apeshit. Kids were spitting at the band, stage-diving, slam-dancing, crowd-surfing, just going crazy. It was like nothing I had ever seen before. I stayed close to my friends. It seemed like complete chaos from afar, but when you got in the middle of it, there was some kind of unwritten code. I did finally go in the pit, mostly because James pushed me into it, and I didn't have a choice. After a few laps around, I noticed that when I fell, complete strangers picked me up and helped me to move onward. I was having fun, and I wasn't even watching the band. I could hear the music loud and clear, and that was good enough for me. I climbed on the stage, and I did my first stage dive. The people in the front caught me, and I surfed on the crowd. IT WAS AWESOME! All the bands were GREAT! I particularly liked T.S.O.L. because they did a song about some kid fucking a dead girl. Also, of course, Dead Kennedys, who blew the roof off the place to close thing out! When I got out of that show, my T-shirt was down around my thighs dripping with sweat. I had bumps and bruises and felt sore all over, but it was the funnest time I had ever had in my life! The Olympic closed its doors to punk shows a few years later in the mid-1980s. In 2005, the Glory Church of Jesus Christ, a Korean-American Christian Church of all things, purchased the entire property. The name Grand Olympic Auditorium no longer exists in Los Angeles except in our memories and some old punk flyers that people saved and post on the Internet. I am forty-nine years old now, and I don't see James that often anymore, but when I do see him, I give him a big hug because I will never forget that night.

Walter Payton, the Banana Boat, and a Fish

It was about midnight on a Wednesday. Mickey and I were playing Tecmo Bowl, a football video game by Nintendo that we had been playing very competitively the past few days. He was always the Pittsburgh Steelers and I, the Oakland Raiders, but tonight that would change. Earlier that day, my little brother had shown me a code that you could enter into the controller that would make *one* player unstoppable—Walter Payton of the Chicago Bears. Mickey, of course, did not know this.

Mickey had been whipping me with the Steelers the past few games and was getting cocky.

"Your ass sucks canal water," he said. I, to this day, still don't know what that means.

"Oh yeah, well, how about one more game?"

"It's your funeral, Jackson!"

"I think I'm gonna try a different team this time."

"Doesn't matter what team you use. I'm still gonna whip your ass!"

This time, instead of the Raiders, I picked the Bears. I pretended to do shitty at first to give him a false sense of hope, and then it was time. Push the red button twice, then the up button, the red button twice again, then the down button. Walter Payton went apeshit! He ran twice as fast as any of Mickey's defensive players. I even ran the wrong way then circled back and still outran his guys for a touchdown.

"What the fuck?" he exclaimed.

"There must be something wrong with the game. It must be broken."

"No, you just suck ass at tackling," I said.

I didn't do it on the next set of downs, again, luring him into thinking it was a fluke. I let him score, and the game was tied. The second time I got the ball, I did the code again. Walter Payton ran circles around his defensive players, and I scored easily again.

"YOU SON OF A BITCH, YOU'RE CHEATING!" he screamed.

"Maybe so, but you're never gonna beat me at this game again."

Then I felt it. SMACK! I saw a bright flash of light, and then for a moment, my head rang.

"What the hell?" I said, not really surprised.

"That's what you get for cheating!" he said.

It took me a second to get my thoughts together after he had sucker punched me in the side of the head, but when I did, I was pissed! We were both sitting on the floor of the living room in front of the TV. There was a coffee table behind us and a couch on our left with an end table next to it with a lamp on it. Mickey must have seen it in my eyes. As he was getting up to run, I pushed him over the couch and end table. He hit the lamp and went crashing to the other side. It made a very loud sound, and the lamp broke into a hundred pieces. Mickey's older sister Cindy came running out of the bedroom where she had been sleeping.

"What the hell's going on in here?" she said

"Mickey was running in the house and he broke the lamp," I said sounding like a child talking to his mother.

"That's not true. Jack pushed me," Mickey said, sounding the same.

"Don't you have a home, Jack?" she asked.

"Now you guys know why we don't have nice things around here. Both of you get out of here right now!"

I met Mickey when we were in seventh grade, the beginning of junior high school. We became best friends when we learned that we were both born on the same day, April 17, in same year, 1968, and lived on the same street, Hopi Road. The only difference was that Mickey lived on Hopi on the west side of Beach Boulevard in the city of Stanton, which was a Mexican gang neighborhood known as Crow Village, and I lived on Hopi on the east side of Beach in the city of Garden Grove, which was a white suburban-type neighborhood. Crow Village was safe for us because we had grown up with most of the gang members that lived there, and even their older brothers, "Veteranos" in Spanish, knew who we were. So any gang member, drug addict, or lowlife who would normally try to kill us left us alone. Hell, even my mom and grandma knew some of their moms and grandmas, so I went way back in the neighborhood even though I didn't live there. All said and done, Mickey was a close friend to my family, as I was to his. I had a secret crush on Mickey's sister Cindy and didn't want to upset her any more than we had already done by waking her up. I grabbed Mickey, and we went out to the garage, planning how I was going to get him back for hitting me.

It was boring in the garage. There was no TV or radio, plus it was the middle of winter, so it was colder than shit! Mickey was pointing his gun at a poster of a girl in a bikini on the wall and taking imaginary target practice at her.

"No one in their right mind would fuck with Miguel Propizaro!" he said.

Miguel Propizaro was a Spanish name he had given himself a few years ago because he was Irish and wanted to sound more Mexican. The problem was that anyone who *would* fuck with us definitely wouldn't be in their right mind to begin with. I happened to look up in the rafters of the garage and saw two fishing poles. One of them was really long. I thought of Indiana Jones and his whip for some reason and thought smacking Mickey across the ass with the pole would be good revenge for him sucker punching me.

"Hey, Miguel, let's take the banana boat and go fishing."

The banana boat was a yellow 1964 Lincoln Continental that he had gotten a few weeks earlier. He showed up at my house one day out of the blue with it.

"Hey, Jack, come outside and check out my new car!"

I walked outside, and there it was. A yellow '64 Continental. It was old and beat-up though and was the ugliest color of yellow I think I had ever seen on a car, and it must have been thirty-five feet long! I had seen these cars in magazines pimped out with black and chrome and nice tires and rims, but this one needed a lot of work. It did have the "suicide doors" on it though, which means that the backdoors were hinged from the back by the rear tire and swung open forward unlike normal car doors. The Mafia used to like these cars because it was easy to get dead bodies in and out of them, and I knew Mickey knew that.

"That thing looks like a goddamn banana boat," I said, hence the name.

"This is the same type of car that President Kennedy got his head blown off in."

"Is famous dead people something that you look for when you're shopping for a car?" I said knowing it was a stupid question.

"Hell ya. This car is cool."

"Well, James Dean was killed in a Porsche Spyder. Is that gonna be the next car you get?"

"Hell no. James Dean puffed the heat seeking moisture missile!"

"What?"

"James Dean was a fag. A homo delecti."

"No, he wasn't. You're thinking of Rock Hudson. He started the AIDS."

"Well, James Dean just died before he could get the AIDS."

"Does this thing have a radio?" I asked.

"Sure does."

"Then let's go for a ride and get some beer."

As we drove down Hopi Road to 7-11, I noticed that the shock absorbers were shot, and the car seemed like it was floating down a river. Up and down and up and down.

"This thing really is a banana boat, isn't it?" I laughed.

I was getting bored of sitting in the garage.

"I heard of a place down in Newport Beach Harbor where you can catch big-ass halibut, but you gotta be careful 'cause it's in a residential part of the marina, and you're not allowed to fish there. Since the rich people don't ever fish in there, these halibut get massive!"

"I don't know," he said.

"Ya, I guess you're right. If you get caught down there, they take you to Newport Jail, and I know you're afraid to go to jail."

I had already been to jail a few times for minor stuff, but I knew Mickey never had, and I was using a kind of child psychology tactic to get his defenses up.

"I'm not afraid to go to jail, you asshole!" Mickey snapped.

We got the fishing poles down from the rafters, and I found an old tackle box with some hooks and sinkers. I grabbed some beer out of the refrigerator in the house, and we loaded the gear into the banana boat. We were going fishing.

We headed south down Beach Boulevard till we got to the ocean and made a left onto PCH (Pacific Coast Highway). A quick pit stop at a bait shop I knew about for salted anchovies and we were on our way.

"We gonna catch some lunkers, Home-Skillet?" he asked me.

"Well, my buddy said he caught some good-sized halibut down by that riverboat using salted anchovies. So we'll see."

"A riverboat?"

"Yah. There's an old riverboat, you know, like they used to have on the Mississippi River for gambling and shit. Well, they built one down in the harbor and turned it into a restaurant. My friend said that's the place to go, *but you got to be quiet!*"

"Why?"

"Because you're not allowed to fish down there and it's a residential area so all the people are sleeping, got it?"

"Yah, I got it, I'll be quiet."

When we got there, it was still dark out. We parked the banana boat and made our way down a steep embankment next to a million-dollar waterfront home there in the marina.

"There aren't any lights on in that house. Maybe they're not home," he said in a whisper.

"Or they're sleeping," I said.

"Either way, if we stay here in the dark and be quiet, we should stay undetected."

We popped open a few beers and started fishing. It was cold and kind of foggy, but it was better than sitting in the garage. I was explaining a certain technique we would use to catch the halibut when it happened. A fished jumped out of the water about ten feet in front of us.

"Did you see that?" Mickey said excitedly.

"Yes, but we are going for halibut and they are on the bottom, so don't worry about that fish."

But it was too late. His ADD was focused on that damn fish. It jumped again.

"There it is again!" he said.

"I'm going to catch him!"

"No, dude. That's probably a mackerel or something. We can't eat those. Leave it alone."

He quickly reeled his line in and cast it in the area the fish had jumped.

"Dude, your line is on the bottom, and that fish is feeding on the surface. You're never gonna catch him. Leave him alone."

"Nah, I'm gonna get him," he said fiendishly.

The fish jumped again.

"That son of a bitch is MOCKING me!"

Now I knew that fish was freaking him out.

The sun was starting to come up, but it was still pretty dark out. He reeled in and cast out a few more times with no luck at hooking his fish.

It jumped again.

"That fish is fucking with the wrong guy! I'm gonna catch him and fry him up for breakfast!"

I could tell that fish was getting to him, so I thought up a task for him to do to get his mind off it.

"My beer's empty. Why don't you go up to the banana boat and get us a few beers?" I said.

My thinking was that a beer would calm him down a little bit. Bad idea. He stomped up the embankment to get the beers. I popped a beer and lit a cigarette thinking of how I was going to get him back for sucker punching me earlier that night. The fish jumped again.

"That's the last straw! I'm gonna teach that motherfucker a lesson!" he yelled.

Then I heard BANG, BANG-BANG-BANG! I was unaware of this, but when I was getting the beers out of the house frig, Mickey had put his handgun in the glove box of the banana boat when he was loading the fishing stuff. When he went up to get the beer, he also grabbed the gun. It was all so surreal! The flash of the shots temporarily blinded me for a second in the darkness, and my ears were ringing because the son of a bitch was standing right next to me after he had handed me my beer.

"That motherfucker fucked with the wrong guys this morning!" he said with a hint of satisfaction in his voice.

"What the hell are you doing, you Irish pig dog? We're supposed to be quiet," I said as my senses where coming back to normal.

"I got him, look!" he said triumphantly.

I looked in the water, and sure enough, he had blown that fish's head off, and its body was floating there in the water. Just then, the lights in the house we were next to came on.

"You woke up the people in the house! Let's get the fuck outta here!"

We got our gear and ran up the embankment to the car. We started the car and got out of there as fast as we could.

"I got him, I got him!" he said excitedly.

"You crazy son of a bitch! We were supposed to be QUIET back there, and you start shooting a gun. This ain't the wild fucking west, we're in Newport fucking Beach!" I said knowing in the back of my mind that the gun was still in his pocket, and he still had two shots left.

"I told that fish he was fucking with the wrong guys!"

"Are you insane? That fish can't hear you. He's underwater!" I said not thinking that the fish couldn't understand English either.

"Give me that gun before you start shooting at birds or some other goddamn thing!"

He gave me the gun, and I felt a little better that I had it because it was still loaded.

"You better hope those people in that house don't call the cops, 'cause if they do we're BOTH going to jail!"

Mike's excitement turned to concern.

"You think so?"

"Hell ya I think so. What do you think?"

"I don't know, Jack. I don't want to go to jail."

"Well, you should have thought about that before you went all medieval on that mackerel."

Things got quiet for a few minutes as we drove. The sun was now up, and I didn't see any cops behind us, so I figured we were in the clear. I could tell that he was scared at the thought of having to go to jail, so I thought I'd try to calm him down a little.

"When I was in high school, I got caught by the Newport Beach cops smoking pot on the beach one morning after surfing, and they took me to their jail. All they did was take my pot away and call my parents to come get me. Before they got there to bail me out, the cops brought me sunrise sandwiches from Carl's Jr. for breakfast! That was so cool because I had the munchies from smoking the weed! So their jail ain't that bad."

"Shit, we'd eat better in there than we would at home," he said sounding a little relieved.

"Damn straight," I said.

Mickey turned on the radio and "The Lemon Song" by Led Zeppelin was playing. He turned it up and started singing the lyrics.

"Squeeze my lemon till the juice runs down my leg. Squeeze my lemon, baby, till the juice runs down my legs."

He stepped on the gas and we drove down PCH, the banana boat floating up and down, up and down, up and down, toward Crow Village.

"I hope your sister isn't up yet. She was pretty mad at us for breaking that lamp last night!"

"Well, let's unload the boat and get all this stuff back in the garage. You grab the beer, and I'll get the poles."

Now this was the time I had been waiting for. My vision of Indiana Jones and his whip the night before was here! I had the gun too. Perfect. As he got the beer and started walking up the front lawn, I struck! Thwack! I whipped him across the ass with the long fishing pole.

"Aaaaaah!" he whined as he went to his knees.

I struck again. Thwack! This time across his back.

"What are you doing? That hurts!" he squealed.

"That's for sucker punching me last night, you asshole. Did you really think I would forget about that? You're lucky I don't shoot you!"

I tried to hit him a third time, but he blocked it with his arm.

"I'm sorry, I'm sorry!" he moaned.

I reached back to thwack him again, but I felt bad and relented. After all, he was my best friend.

I got into my car and headed home.

I pulled up to my place, parked, and walked up the driveway into the house. I went into my bedroom and laid on the bed. I felt something poking my belly and reached into the front pocket of the hooded sweater

I was wearing. I still had the pistol Mickey had given me earlier. I checked the chamber, yep, two bullets left. I thought, that crazy son of a bitch, as I pictured him shooting at that poor fish. I hid the gun in the sock drawer of my dresser and lay back down in my bed. It had been a long night, and I was very tired. It would be nice to get a few hours of sleep. Just then the phone rang. *Shit, what now?* I thought.

"Hello?" I asked.

"Jackson, it's Mickey."

"What do you want?" I said trying to sound more tough than tired.

"I wanted to say that I'm sorry for punching you last night. It wasn't right for me to hit you when you weren't looking, brotha."

"Don't worry about it, dude. You hit like a girl anyway. I caught it on the side of the head, so I don't even think I'll get a black eye. I'm sorry for whipping you with the fishing pole," I said, after all he was my brother from another mother.

"That's okay. I deserved it. Come over later, if you want. I'm gonna go to the store and get some halibut and have a fish fry."

"Okay, brother, I'm gonna get some sleep for a few hours. I'll give you a call." Then I hung up the phone.

I laid there for a few minutes and then thought, *Mickey was right. That fish did fuck with the wrong two guys this morning.* I smiled as I fell asleep.

Highway 39 Drive-In

The Highway 39 drive-in movie theater was located in Westminster, California. It was built in 1955 and was the largest drive-in theater in Southern California. It had a 1,600-car capacity and three movie screens that were almost ten stories high each. If you were a kid growing up in Orange County, this place was awesome! My family moved from Los Angeles to Anaheim in 1971. My parents loved movies and immediately fell in love with the theater, so we would go there all the time.

A night at the drive-in would start with my mom heating up a few Jiffy Pop popcorns on the stove. Jiffy Pop was a brand of popcorn that came in what I would describe as an aluminum pie tin with a handle. Inside the tin were the corn kernels and butter. Over the tin was a spiraled piece of tin foil. As the stove heated the bottom of the pie tin, the kernels would start to pop, in turn making the foil rise into a domelike shape. After all the kernels were popped, you could then tear open the foil and eat the popcorn. I used to love to watch my mom heat up these things. It was fascinating to me. Like science or something. I couldn't wait to be old enough to be able to cook one myself. Unfortunately, with the mass production in microwave ovens later in the decade, Jiffy Pop stopped making the pie tin–style popcorn packaging. My mom would tear open the foil at the top, and steam would billow out of the hole filling the kitchen with the smell of hot buttered popcorn. She would then pour it into a brown paper grocery bag. After that, my dad would go out to the garage and get out the old metal Coleman cooler. We'd fill it with cans of soda, plastic bowls, and ice.

With my little brother and I already dressed in our slippers and pajamas, we were now ready to go! It was just a short drive down Beach Boulevard (Highway 39), and we were there. My dad would always like to get there early so we could try out a few different parking spots. It was important to find one with a good working speaker, otherwise the movie would sound like shit. Once he found one that was acceptable, my brother and I would run off to the playground that they had built right underneath the screen. We would play with all the other kids in their pajamas until it got dark and the movie began. With everybody safely back in the car, my dad would roll down the window of the old Ford Station Wagon, hook the speaker on the edge of the window, and turn the speaker on. First, the "Take a Trip to the Snack Bar" song would play on the huge movie screen. Next, if it was a kids' movie, they would play a few Disney or Looney Tunes cartoons. When the cartoons would start, my dad would take us out of the backseat and lift us up so we could sit on the roof of the car. My mom would hand us a can of soda and a bowl of popcorn, and we would stay up there all night. The best seats in the house! I never thought about this as a kid, but this would also give my parents the privacy to do whatever they wanted to do inside the car as well. It was great to be a kid in Orange County, California, back in the 1970s. My brother and I used to have a blast together even when we got in trouble; we were thick as thieves.

I continued to go there once I got my driver's license and car in the 1980s. I would go on dates with girls or sneak in alcohol and pot and party with my friends. We once got drunk and went down to the old playground and started monkeying around until the security guards came over and kicked us out. In the 1990s, I even took my own daughter there to see movies a few times. That made it a full circle. I went there with my parents, and she went there with her parents. They tore the old place down in 1997. The last two features they played were Howard Stern's movie *Private Parts* and *Beavis and Butthead Do America*. It's been replaced by a Wal-Mart now. Go figure. I had a lot of great times at the Highway 39 over the decades, but my favorite memories would still have to be going there as a kid. The place was magical to me. I will never forget those nights at the drive-in, eating popcorn with my brother in our pajamas and watching movies with my family. I'm a very lucky man.

The Neighbor Next Door

I was finally approved to move into my new apartment. It was a two-bedroom, one-bath, a quarter of a mile away from the beach, and close to my daughter's school. Perfect! It also had a washer and dryer in the kitchen area, which I loved. I hated having to share the washroom with the other tenants at my last place and having to pay for it with quarters. The only thing I didn't like about it is that my front door was basically right on the street. Outside was my porch and a very small lawn, then the public sidewalk, a little more grass, then the street. So anybody walking down the sidewalk could look right inside my apartment. Over the next couple of days, my daughter and I got all moved in and settled.

The first time I saw him, I was going out to get the mail. My apartment was at the corner of the complex, and the mailboxes were on the wall outside my living room. Between my complex and the other complex to the south was a brick wall. So basically, even though we didn't live in the same apartment buildings, he was my closest neighbor. I got my mail and turned around. He was smoking a cigarette. He looked at me and gave me a kind of nod, like "welcome to the neighborhood." He was small and thin with messy blond hair. The basic Huntington Beach surfer look. I nodded back and walked into my place. I didn't like making new friends or talking to strangers.

It was a nice morning, so I decided to go for a jog to the beach. I was stretching outside my front door, and I saw him smoking a cigarette out on his porch. As I ran south past his place, I waved.

"You know, those things will kill ya," I said jokingly.

He just smiled and nodded his head as if to say "I know."

That was the first time I had seen him since the day at the mailboxes. It was also the first time I had ever talked to him. I jogged to the beach, and by the time I got back, he was gone.

It was a few days later; I was on my way home from work. It was getting late, so my daughter and I picked up some fast food for dinner. I pulled up to my place and parked my truck. My daughter got out before me to go unlock the front door while I grabbed the food. As I was walking up to my door, I saw him out of the corner of my eye.

"Now that stuff will kill ya, you know," he said with a big smile.

"Give me convenience or give me death!" I yelled back.

When I got into the apartment, my daughter asked me.

"Who are you talking to, Daddy?"

"The guy next door."

"What guy?"

"Our neighbor. He's smoking out on his porch."

My daughter went and looked out the door.

"There's nobody over there," she said.

"Well, he must have gone in. Now get over here and get your food before it gets cold."

That weekend, my daughter had a sleepover at one of her friends' houses, so I had some time to go out. I went to a few bars downtown and saw some friends. It was about 1:00 a.m. when I got home, and I was pretty buzzed up. I walked by his apartment, and, of course, he was out there smoking. I stumbled up on his lawn.

"How's it goin'?" I said drunkenly.

"I'm doing good. How are you?" he replied.

"I'm fine."

"Looks like you were out having some fun tonight."

"Yeah, I've had a few drinks." I pulled a cigarette out and lit it.

"So you smoke too. I thought you didn't approve."

"I smoke mostly when I drink. It's a bad habit."

"My name is Chuck. So what do they call you?"

"I'm Jack. It's nice to finally meet you, Chuck. Sorry, I'm drunk."

"That's okay. I like to throw a few back myself every once in a while."

"Cool, well, we'll have to do that then."

"What do you do for a living? You get home pretty late in the evening sometimes." He lit up another cigarette.

"I'm a commodities broker, so I work long hours most of the week. What do you do?"

"I'm unemployed at the moment, but I'm sure I'll find some work here real soon," he said enthusiastically.

"I'm sure you will."

"Well, since I'm here all day, I'll keep an eye on your place. Make sure everything is cool over there while you are at work."

"I appreciate that, Chuck. Now I have to go in and lay down for a while. You have a good night."

"You too, man," he said kind of chuckling to himself.

That Monday morning, I thought about Chuck and how he needed a job. I went to the human resources department of my firm. Maybe I could get Chuck a job as a telemarketer or something like that. I asked our HR lady if anything was available. She said we hadn't hired anybody in months. I thought that at least I had tried, and as long as he was unemployed, he was keeping an eye on my place. So that wasn't bad. That night when I got home, he was outside.

"Hey, Chuck! How was the job hunting today?" I said with hope.

"Not so good, but I'll be back at it again tomorrow."

"Well, I checked with my HR department for you today, but my firm isn't hiring right now. Sorry."

"That's okay. I'll find some work here real soon," he said with a sad smile.

"All right. I'll see you tomorrow, buddy."

"I have a good feeling that things are gonna get a lot better around here real soon. You have a good night now, Jack," he said confidently.

I was sitting in my living room, and I started wondering how he could afford his rent over there. And how he always had cigarettes. I had been living there for about a month already. Oh well, he must be on unemployment or disability or something like that. Hopefully he will find a job soon.

I didn't see Chuck for the rest of the week. Saturday morning, I woke up to a commotion going on next door. I got out of bed and looked out my window. There was a big moving van parked out in front of my apartment.

Shit, I thought.

Apparently, Chuck couldn't find a job, so he has to move out of his place. That's fucked up. Well, the least I can do is help him put his stuff in the van. So I got dressed and walked outside. There were two girls out there getting furniture out of the van and moving it into the apartment.

"Hey there, ladies. What's going on?" I said very confused.

"We're moving in next door. We are your new neighbors!" The blonde one said excitedly.

"Well, where's Chuck?"

"Who's Chuck?" the brunette replied.

"The guy who lives there."

"No one lives there, silly. We signed a six-month lease a month ago, and today is the first, so we're moving in. Isn't that exciting?" Blondie said in a high-pitched voice.

"Well, let me help you with that table."

I picked up the table and walked over to Chuck's front door. As I walked in, the apartment was empty. I realized that I had never been in there before. I put down the table and checked out the rest of the place. Fucking empty!

"Are you sure there wasn't anyone living here when you signed the lease?"

"No, we're positive. When the manager showed us the apartment, it was empty," Blondie said.

"Where's the manager's office? I have something I want to ask him real quick."

"Around the corner in the front of the building. Is everything all right?"

"Oh yes, everything is fine. The guy that lived here before you was a friend of mine, so I just want to see if he left a forwarding address. I'll be right back."

I walked over to the manager's office. Thank God he was there. I went in and introduced myself.

"Hello, my name is Jack. Are you the manager?'

"Yes, I am. Can I help you?"

"Well, I live in the apartments next door, and I see that you have some new tenants moving in."

"That is correct. Today is the first of the month. Is there a problem?"

"No, not at all. I was just wondering if there was a guy named Chuck living there before they moved in."

His face changed completely.

"There was a gentleman named Charles Harris that lived there. Were you two friends?" he said cautiously.

"Well, kind of. I just never had a chance to say good-bye, so I was wondering if he left a forwarding address."

"I'm sorry, Jack, but Charles is no longer with us."

"What do you mean he's no longer with us? Do you mean he's dead?"

"Yes, I'm afraid so."

"What happened to him?"

"Well, Mr. Harris lost his job and was unable to pay his rent for two months. The owner of the building told me to me to get the money for the back rent or I had to evict him."

"He wasn't able to get the money, I take it," I said feeling very sad.

"No, he wasn't, so I had to give him an eviction notice. After that, he got very depressed. I went to check on him a few days later, and he didn't answer the door. I used my master key to enter his apartment and found him on the floor of the living room with a pill bottle next to him. He apparently overdosed on pills."

"So he committed suicide?" I said.

"According to the paramedics, yes."

"Wow, that's terrible. I had no idea."

"Yes, it is very unfortunate."

"Okay, well, thank you for your time."

I walked around the corner and back to Chuck's place. The girls were inside, so I ran over to my apartment and ducked inside. I went to the fridge and popped open a beer. I sat down and started putting the pieces together. Okay, so I talked to him, but I never touched him. He always wore a white T-shirt and black shorts. I just thought maybe he had a lot of white shirts that's not out of the ordinary. Then I remembered that when he was out there smoking, his front door was never open. It was always closed. Even at night when it was cold he would never go in and put a jacket on, and his porch light was never on either. He would just stand there and smoke in the dark. When I told him I couldn't get him a job at my work, that was the last time I talked to him. He told me that things were going to get a lot better around here. Those where the last words he said to me.

I heard laughing and screaming coming from the front yard. I went to the window and looked through the blinds. Betty and Veronica had put on bikini tops and were using my hose to squirt each other with water. I just stood there watched them for a minute. They were both gorgeous! Chuck was right. Things did get a lot better around there that day. I walked back outside to see if they still needed help moving in to their exciting new apartment. They did. You did a good job keeping an eye on the place, Chuck. Thank you, buddy.

Henry Winkler, Famous Rock Star

I was sitting at home watching TV and drinking beer dreading having to go to work at the steel yard the next day when my phone rang.

"Hello," I said.

"JB, what are you doing?" It was my girlfriend Julie.

"Drinking beer and watching TV. Why?"

"Well, me and my sisters just got back from the store, and we got a bottle of Jack Daniels, and it made me think of you. Why don't you come over and drink it with us?"

"Julie, you live all the way out in Hollywood. I'm not going to drive all the way up there just because you bought a bottle of Jack. I can go to the liquor store on the corner here and have one in five minutes. Besides, I have to work in the morning."

"Ah come on, pleeeeze, I miss you. You can spend the night with me and then go to work from here. Anyway, I live closer to the steel yard than you do."

She had a point. The steel yard I worked at is in the city of Vernon, in south central Los Angeles, which is a lot closer to Hollywood than where I live in Huntington Beach.

"I don't know, babe," I said already knowing I was going to go.

"After we get drunk and go to bed I'll speak French to you the whole time we're having sex like you like," she said in a teasingly sexy voice, also already knowing I was going.

Okay, here's the deal with Julie. She lives in a house off Sunset Boulevard with her two sisters on Ogden Drive in Hollywood. The house was supposedly owned by Lucille Ball in the 1950s, but this was never confirmed. All three of them are super-hot. Julie is tall with long, long legs, light brown hair down below the middle of her back, not an ounce of fat on her, and is *always* happy, which can be annoying at times. She is the type of girl who will do *anything* at the drop of a hat and loved to drink. She'll show up at your door out of the blue with a bottle of booze at three o'clock in the morning on a Tuesday night with a pink wig on ready to party like it's nothing. Or we'll be having breakfast in the morning, and she'll say, "Let's go to Vegas! I'll drive," and off we'd go to Vegas. Shit like that. She said she and her sisters grew up in Oklahoma and were raised by their aunt and uncle, who were American Indians, because her parents died. She went to a university in France for two years and spoke fluent French. She was very wild, but book-smart, and I had no clue how they got to Hollywood. Are you as confused as I am? It gets better. She is only in her very early twenties but is already some kind of executive at a major computer company and works in their corporate office, which was in a high-rise in downtown LA. She had a brand-new black Mercedes-Benz and pays for the house they lived in and lets her sisters live there for free. That's my Julie.

"Okay, baby, I'm leaving in five minutes."

"Oh YAY! I knew you'd come. Jack's coming, you guys. I told you he'd come over. I miss him sooooo much!" I could hear her say to her sisters before I hung up the phone.

Keep in mind I had just seen her a few days before, so it wasn't like I hadn't seen her in a long time; she is just always excited and happy. That's just the way she is.

I got in my car and headed north on the 5 Freeway to the 101 Freeway and got off on Sunset. Headed west on Sunset toward Ogden Drive to Julie, her two hot sisters, and *my* fifth of JD which I had instructed her *not* to open until I got there. As I was driving down Sunset, I had to take a piss. I left in a hurry thinking about her talking in French to me and that bottle of Jack and forgot to take a piss. I had already drunk a lot of beer at home and was feeling a little buzzed. I looked at my gas gauge, and it was almost on empty, so I pulled in to an ARCO gas station for gas, beer, and a pee. I parked my car at pump number one and got out. As I got out, I stepped in gum some asshole had spit on the ground before I got there.

"Shit!" I said scraping the bottom of my shoe on the curb of the island the pump was on to get the gum off. I was pissed.

"Can I wash your windshield, sir?" There was a homeless black guy walking up to me.

"Did you spit this fucking gum on the ground?" I said disgusted.

"No, sir. Did you step in gum?"

"Ya, some asshole spit gum on the ground, and now it's all over my shoe."

"I'm sorry, sir. Can I wash your windows? I usually charge $5, but since you stepped in the gum, I'll do it for $2."

"No, I'm good, thanks. I'm in a hurry."

I walked into the station and asked for the restroom key and then went into the restroom to take a piss. After I was done, I took the key and scraped the gum off my shoe with it. I went back to the mini mart, got some beer, and put $20 on pump number one. As I walked back to my car, I noticed a black BMW was behind me at pump number two. The actor Henry Winkler was pumping gas into the beemer and talking to the homeless guy. Now I am terrible at noticing famous people in person (a) because they don't really look the same as they do in the movies or on TV in person and (b) because I really don't give a fuck, so I don't pay attention to people that much. Julie, on the other hand, was a professional goddamn celebrity spotter and would always get starstruck and point out every famous actor or actress or rock star or whoever to me and then walk up and talk to them like she knew them. I always HATED this because she would introduce me to them like they should know me, which would sometimes confuse them. This was actually funny because I had long hair down to my waist, and she was smoking hot, so they would think

I was a rock star but not really know which band I was in. Hilarious, huh? Anyway, I would just stand there and act bored, which I was, and eventually they would find an excuse to get away from her. When I was a kid, my mom took my brother and I with my cousins to see a taping of the TV show *Happy Days*. After the show, she bought us all Fonzie T-shirts with a picture of Henry Winkler on the front flipping his thumbs up and saying "Haaayyy," which was his trademark on the show. Since I had seen him at the show, I recognized him at the pump behind me. He gave the homeless guy some money, and he feverishly began washing his windows. After the homeless guy was done, he got into his car and drove away down Sunset. I was still pumping my gas when the black guy walked up to me.

"Did you see that?" he said all excited.

"See what?" I said knowing better than to talk to him.

"Arthur Fonzarelli just gave me $10 to wash his windows."

"That wasn't Arthur Fonzarelli."

"Sure the hell was! Haaayyy!" he said flipping his thumbs in the air.

"That was Henry Winkler."

"Henry who? Henry Winkelli?"

"Henry Winkler is his name. Arthur Fonzarelli is just the character he played on TV."

"Naw man, I don't know who this Henry guy you're talking about is, but Arthur Fonzarelli just gave me $10 to wash his windows!"

"Never mind," I said.

"Hey, you're famous too, aren't you? Let me wash your windows."

"I'm not famous."

"Ya, you look like that one guy in that one rock band. You a rock star?"

"No, I'm not that guy."

"Well, you sure do look like him!" he said excitedly.

I was done pumping my gas. I reached in my car and grabbed a beer out of the bag.

"You got me, brother. My name is Henry, Henry Winkler, and I *am* a famous rock star," I said with a big smile.

"I knew you was him! I knew it," he said reaching out his hand.

"Don't need my windows washed because I just had my car detailed, but here's a beer, man." I handed him the beer and shook his hand.

"Thank you, sir. Man, what a day! Two famous people come through my gas station at the same time. Arthur Fonzarelli and Henry Winkelli! Now I got $10 and a beer."

"Maybe one day I'll write a song about this, huh?" I said.

"Yes sir, that would be sumptin'!"

"Well, enjoy that beer. I gotta go."

I got into my car and pulled out onto Sunset Boulevard. As I drove, I thought that Julie will be so excited! She gets to sleep with the famous rock star Henry Winkler tonight! The sun was setting just above the Hollywood Hills. I flipped down my sun visor and grabbed a beer out of the bag and opened it. I took a good drag and placed it between my legs. Julie was waiting.

A Suicidal Failure

I woke up very early yesterday morning. The sun was just peeking over the horizon. I could hear the birds starting to sing outside my window and a dog barking in the distance. I lay there thinking about my life. I have no job, no woman, no money, and no family. Nothing really to speak of but heartache and despair. I can't afford my rent, so at the end of the month, I will lose my apartment and be homeless. So I decided that day would be the last day of my life.

I would do all my favorite things. Kind of a last hurrah to celebrate my shitty life. I got out of bed and walked over to my bookshelf. I pulled out a Charles Bukowski book and began reading some of his short stories. In one of the stories, he was taking a bath. I haven't taken a bath in years, so I would start my day with a bath instead of a shower. I ran the water as hot as I could and got in. It felt good. The bathtub was a little small for me, so I put my feet up on the side of the tub. I thought to myself that I could just dunk my head under the water and drown myself right then and there. I had too many things that I wanted to do though. The day was young. I had the whole day to figure out how I was going to do myself in!

After my bath, I got out and towcled off. I opened the window and looked out. There were clouds in the sky, and it looked like it was going to rain. I thought of Black Sabbath's first album. On the first song, it starts off with rain and a bell tolling in the distance. I went to my turntable and put on that record. Then I went to my dresser and got out my old "Ozzy" cross and put it on. I got it out of an Ozzy Osbourne box set I bought years ago. So far I have read my favorite author and listened to my favorite band, and it's not even noon yet! I walked over to my closet, took out my best suit, and laid it on the bed. I only wore this suit to job interviews and funerals. Since it was going to be my final day on Earth, it seemed appropriate. Next, I needed shoes. I looked at the pairs I had, and they were all old and worn. None of them went with my suit. I got the idea that if none of my shoes matched my suit, then today I wound not wear shoes at all. I would go barefoot.

Instead of eating breakfast, I elected to drink. I had some beers in the refrigerator, so I grabbed one and popped it open. I felt nice and cold going down. I liked the idea of drinking this early in the morning and remembered that the bar on the corner opened at 6:00 a.m. That will be the first place I would go. Wearing no shoes, I walked over to the corner bar. I knew the bartender there, and she knew me. We didn't like each other very much but tolerated one another. I ordered a shot of Jack Daniels and a pint of Budweiser. Now I didn't have any cash, but I did have a credit card. The card was maxed out, though. I gave her the card and told her to just hold it, and I would pay in cash when I was done. She put it on a clipboard next to the cash register. She asked me why I had no shoes on, but I just ignored her. I could see her shake her head in disapproval out of the corner of my eye. I ordered six pints of beer and six shots of whiskey in a relatively short amount of time, so I was starting to get drunk. It was late morning, and the regular drunks started coming in for their breakfast. This would be a nice time for my exit. I told the bartender that I had to go and to just put it on the credit card. She ran the card and told me it wouldn't accept the charge. I told her to run it again, knowing damn well there was no credit left on it. She ran it again. Of course, it didn't work again. I could see the bouncer sitting in the corner get up from his stool. The bartender motioned over to him. He started walking toward me.

"Listen, buddy, if you don't have the cash, we're gonna have to call the cops," he said trying his best to sound tough.

"Oh, I have the cash right here." I put my hand in my pocket and made a fist.

When he got close enough I pulled my fist out of my pocket and punched him as hard as I could right in the face. To my amazement, I knocked him out! I guess he wasn't so tough after all. I turned and ran out the door. It was cold out and I didn't have shoes on, but it seemed like I could run faster without them. I turned down the alley like a sharp-dressed cat and headed for home. As I ran, I remembered that I opened my bathroom window after I got out of the bathtub to look outside. If it was still open, I could get into my apartment through the back alley. I got to the back of my place, and thank God it was still open. I took the screen off and wiggled myself through the small window. After I was safely inside, I thought, *Wow, that was exciting.* I had never done anything like that before. I went to the fridge and grabbed another beer. What should I do next?

I looked to the corner of my room and saw my guitar. It was a 1968 Gibson SG. I had bought it at a pawnshop when I was a teenager over thirty years ago. It was my prized possession. The only thing I had that was worth anything. If I could only play it one last time. I didn't have an amplifier, though. Then it came to me! I could take it to a pawnshop and pretend like I'm going to sell it. They have amps there that I could plug into. Genius! I grabbed the guitar, put it in its case, and out the door I went. I was glad the pawnshop was in the opposite direction from the bar. Getting arrested would fuck up my plans to kill myself. When I got to the shop, it was already afternoon. I walked in and asked the owner if he'd like to buy it. Of course he did. It was all original hardware and pickups with the original guitar case. He offered me three grand for it right off the bat. I asked him if he would like to hear it. He took me over to where the amplifiers were, and I plugged her in. She sounded great! Like the first time I bought her. I hit a low E chord and turned the amp up.

"What do you think?" I said smiling ear to ear.

"I think it sounds great. So do we have a deal?"

"Well, now that I'm hearing it through this Marshall amplifier I think I'm getting cold feet about selling it."

"I can see that," he said looking down at my bare feet.

"Take your time thinking about it and I'll be over at the counter if you change your mind."

My plan worked! I sat there and played my SG for about fifteen to twenty minutes. As I left the shop, I told the owner that maybe I would sell it to him another time.

Back in my apartment, I thought about what I wanted for my last meal. Steak was always my favorite thing to eat, so steak it would be. Luckily, I had bought one a few days ago, and it was marinating in my fridge. I grabbed another beer and turned on the television. To my amazement, the last episode of the last season of "Breaking Bad" was just starting. That was my favorite TV show. I love how at the end Walter White goes out in a blaze of glory. Killing everyone around him, including himself. I couldn't go out like that, though. I'm too much of a coward. I don't want it to hurt. At that moment, I decided to take pills. Overdosing on pills wouldn't hurt at all. You just go to sleep and never wake up.

After the TV show, it was starting to get late. I went into the kitchen and started cooking my steak. While it was cooking, I looked through my DVDs to find a final movie to watch. I pulled out *Fast Times at Ridgemont High.* I loved that movie and figured watching a comedy from my childhood would be nice before I hit the "big sleep." I finished my dinner and movie. Now it was time to end it all. In the kitchen, I had half a bottle of whiskey. I took the whiskey from the shelf and walked into the bathroom. In the medicine cabinet, I had half a bottle of sleeping pills. I figured with all the beer and booze I had drunk during the day, mixed with the pills, would do me in. I took all the pills and washed them down with all the whiskey. I went over and grabbed my guitar and laid it on the bed. At least I would not die alone. I laid on my bed next to the guitar and closed my eyes. I was feeling really cold and tired. I could hear it start raining outside. I thought about my last girlfriend and how beautiful her smile was. I thought about Hunter S. Thompson and how the last words on his suicide note said "This won't hurt" before he blew his brains out, but I'm sure it did. I will not leave a note. Deep down I don't really care how people feel about me because I am shallow. I only care about myself. Anyway, the only people who would read the note would be the cops. I lit up a last cigarette, and then I was out.

When I awoke this morning, I was still alive. The pills and the whiskey were not enough to kill me. I guess my tolerance was too high. As I looked down to my right, I noticed that I had passed out with a lit cigarette and a small fire had burned my carpet and my nightstand, but didn't catch onto the rest of the apartment. I was a suicidal failure two times over last night. I couldn't even burn down my apartment properly. What a pisser. I guess I will have to try and kill myself again another day.

Social Media Junkie

Joey was addicted to Facebook. He would be on there from the time he woke up in the morning till the time he went to bed at night. He did stop to sleep, but he hardly ever logged off. Even when he would eat, he would take a picture of his food in the hopes of getting a couple of "likes." He had the limit of five thousand friends on the website but only really knew about five of them. He had no real friends or family. He literally lived his life through his computer. Joey was a social media junkie. He liked to follow people's day whether it be at work, at home, or when they were out and about. He had a few favorites, but Christa was by far his number one! He followed her on Facebook all the time. The funny thing about this was that she didn't even know he existed. She had accepted his friend request a few years ago and thought nothing of it at the time. She never commented on or liked any of his posts, but unknowingly she had just invited a stalker into her life. Joey would start off in the morning following her timeline to see what she had for breakfast and that she got to work okay. Once at work, she would usually post a funny meme about her boss or her cat that he would laugh at hysterically. After work, he would always try to find out what she was having for dinner. He would then try to replicate it and eat the same thing. He would fantasize that they were on a date. Talking and laughing and having a wonderful time. At night, he had a special pillow that he would snuggle up with and say, "Good night, Christa" to it before he fell asleep. This was all perfectly normal to him. After all, nobody knew he was doing it, especially Christa.

The next morning was a Saturday, and Joey did the usual routine. He knew what time Christa usually woke up, so he would get up a little earlier, wash up and eat, then wait for her to log on. Today she was meeting her sister and a few of her girlfriends for lunch. The restaurant was right down the street from Joey's apartment. He thought how great it would be to see her in person, so he made plans to go down there at around noon. When he got there, he took a seat at the corner of the bar. From this vantage point, he could see the whole dining room clearly. The place wasn't that big, so it started to fill up fast. Pretty soon, it was packed with people, and there was nowhere to sit at the bar. He held his seat on the corner. Finally, Christa and her friends came in. She looked beautiful in her white summer dress and sandals. She had straightened her hair, which is just the way he liked it. It was almost like she knew he would be there, but of course, she didn't. Joey smiled as they were seated at a perfect table for him to watch them. He ordered another drink from the bartender and settled in. There were four of them. The one on the left must be Christa's sister because they looked alike, but he wasn't sure. He couldn't hear what they were saying but imagined that he was sitting at their table, engaging them with witty conversation. They would all laugh, and Christa would give her sister a look like "He's mine." Just then, Christa got up from the table and started walking right toward him. Beads of sweat ran down his forehead. He tried not to look nervous. What would he tell her? As she walked past him, he realized that the women's restroom was right behind him at the back of the bar. *Whew!* he thought. That was a close one. If she ever found out who he was, his cover would be blown. Then he couldn't appreciate her up close like he was today. Eventually she would recognize him, and everything would be ruined. He was about to order another drink from the bartender when he felt a little nudge on his right side. It was Christa. She was done in the restroom and had gone to the bar to place an order.

"Can I get a pitcher of margaritas, please," she said with the voice of an angel.

He could smell the scent of the shampoo she had used to wash her hair in the shower just hours before. He had to be cool, so he just looked straight ahead.

"How are you doing today?" Christa smiled as she waited for her pitcher.

"Um, I'm okay I guess" were the first words he spoke to the love of his life!

"It's such a nice day, isn't it?"

"Um, yeah, I guess," Joey said trying not to look nervous.

"I'm Christa. What's your name?"

"I'm Joey."

"Well, it's good to meet you, Joey."

"It's good to finally meet you." He didn't mean to say it that way, but that's how it came out.

"Hey, don't I know you from somewhere?" She didn't catch it.

"I don't think so."

"Yeah, I think we're friends on Facebook." She pulled out her phone.

"Maybe."

"I knew it. There you are right there. See I told you we were friends." She showed him his home page.

"That must have been from a long time ago."

"Sometimes you post funny stuff!" She looked a little buzzed.

"Do you ever like my posts?" He already knew that she didn't.

"I think I do," she replied.

Just then her pitcher of margaritas arrived. Joey just sat petrified there not knowing what to say. Christa still had her phone in her hand.

"Well, I have to take this pitcher over to my table now. You know what? We should take a selfie together!" She put her arm around his neck, reached out her right hand, and, click, took their picture.

"It was nice meeting you, Joey!" She spun around in that gorgeous dress and floated back to her table like a ghost.

Joey could not believe what just happened! He actually met Christa. She touched him. They took a fucking selfie together! He couldn't wait to get home to see if she posted it. He paid his bar tab and got out of there. When he got home, he immediately got on the computer, but Christa hadn't posted anything yet. They must have still been at the bar. He waited all day into the night. Finally, he curled up with his pillow and fell asleep.

The next morning, he got up and logged on to Facebook. He was thinking that he didn't want to get too excited just in case she didn't post their picture. He clicked on her homepage, and sure enough, there were pictures. Quite a few of them. It looks like the girls had a pretty crazy night! The photos started out at Christa's apartment with her sister and her friends. There was one out in front of the restaurant. Then there it was. Their selfie. She did post it after all. He was so proud! He wanted to open his window and scream to the world how much he loved her. He immediately downloaded the picture to his computer and printed it out. Then he carefully taped it to the mirror over his dresser. It came out perfect. He wanted to share it to his page for all to see. He leapt over to his computer, but he couldn't do it. He just couldn't. They had just met, and he didn't want her to know that he had been stalking her. His pride turned to shame. With a shaking index finger, he gently clicked "like" on the photo, and that was that.

A few days passed before Joey started to Facebook-follow her again. It was very hard for him to even wait that long, but he did. The first thing he noticed was that her relationship status had changed from "Single" to "It's Complicated." Could she be talking about him? He began to get very excited and scrolled through her timeline but couldn't really find anything. He clicked on her photos and scrolled back to Saturday. It was now Wednesday, so he had to go back a couple of days but he found them. There was around twenty pictures in the album. Their selfie was about in the middle. As he continued on, a guy entered the scene. He was tall with dark brown hair. The guy and Christa seemed to be getting very close. The last photo was them embracing with a kiss. This upset Joey greatly. He felt like throwing up. He placed his face in his hands and started to cry. It seems that after he left her on Saturday, she met a guy. Over the days that he had quit Facebook stalking her, they had hooked up. How could she do this to him? They had just met. She didn't even give him a chance! He picked up his computer and smashed it to the ground. From now on, he would not let her out of his sight!

Jocy was in a rage. Not really thinking clearly, he went back to the restaurant where they had met. Of course, she wasn't there, and he felt stupid. That pissed him off even more. He logged on to Facebook, and her status showed where she worked and the address. It was a start. As he arrived, her shift was just getting off for the night. Then he just followed her home. It was that easy. Now he knew where she worked and where she lived. He sat there in his car for a while. He was just about to leave when a car pulled into her driveway. It was the guy from the pictures. The guy got out of his car and walked into her apartment without even knocking on the door. Joey looked down, and he had a rather large hunting knife that he kept for protection. He had bought it at a swap meet about a year ago. It felt good in his hand. He got out of the car and slowly walked across the street. He heard arguing and snuck over to a window. He couldn't hear what they were saying, but just then he heard a crash. Like something had broken on the floor. Joey raced over to the front door, knife in hand. He was going to protect his love from this asshole. The door was still unlocked, and Joey burst in. They were standing in the living room arguing loudly, so they didn't see him at first. The guy had his back to Joey, so he crept up behind him and plunged the knife deep into his back. He pulled it out and did it again. Christa had a look of horror on her face. Just for good measure, he stabbed him a third time.

"What are you doing?" Christa screamed.

"I came to save you."

"Save me from what?"

"From him." Joey pointed proudly, almost smiling.

"He's my ex-boyfriend. We were just having a harmless argument. Are you crazy?"

"I thought he was going to hurt you."

"He would never hurt me. He loves me. Who the hell are you?"

"Joey. I'm Joey"

"That guy from the bar last week?"

"Yes, remember we took a selfie together."

"Why are you here?"

"Because I love you, Christa."

Christa knelt down and picked her ex-boyfriend's limp lifeless body up onto her lap.

"Fuck you, you fucking asshole! I don't even know you." She got out her phone, the same one she took their picture with and dialed 911.

"Hello, operator, I need an ambulance!"

Joey slumped down into a chair and slowly dropped the knife onto the floor. Christa scurried over on her hands and knees and grabbed the knife. She pointed it at him with her hands trembling with fear, her boyfriend's blood all over her work clothes. Joey could hear the police sirens getting closer. He had made a terrible mistake.

They took Joey to the station and questioned him. He told them everything. About the social media stalking, how they met, and that he was guilty of murder. They questioned Christa too. Even though she didn't really know why all this happened to her, she did remember meeting him at the bar, and the cops took the selfie as evidence. The ex-boyfriend went straight to the morgue. He was DOA. Didn't even stand a chance being ambushed from behind like that. Joey was put in a cell by himself. As the officer put him in the cell and locked the door, he told Joey this:

"You know, kid, I was the one that interviewed the girl in there. She told me that she was breaking up with that guy you killed because things weren't working out between them. That's why they were arguing. She also told me that after they broke up, she was going to ask *you* if you wanted to go out with her this weekend. I guess you fucked that all up now, didn't you? Have a good night."

Joey just sat there. He couldn't believe it. All he had to was leave her alone, and they would have had a date this weekend. The cop was absolutely right. He did fuck it all up. Now he would never see the girl of his dreams again. He closed his eyes and started fantasizing about how wonderful their date would have been. Where would they go? Would they hold hands? Would they kiss?

The next morning, the guards came in to give him his breakfast, but Joey wasn't hungry. He was hanging dead in his cell. He had taken his bedsheets and tied them all together to make a noose. The guards rushed to open the door and cut his body down, but it was too late. Joey was dead. He couldn't even bear the thought of going one day without his love. The guard took the sheet from around his neck, and as he did, he noticed some writing on the wall. Inside a big heart, it said "Joey and Christa Forever."

You can still go on Joey's Facebook page to this day because no one ever even cared enough about him to deactivate it.

Driving Under the Influence

4-12-1989:

It was five days before my twenty-first birthday.

7:30 p.m.: I drive to Sound Factory Studios on Beach Boulevard and Chapman Avenue. I park and unload my guitar, amplifier, and other equipment.

7:50 p.m.: I walk to the liquor store and purchase a twelve-pack of Budweiser.

8:05 p.m.: We warm up and I practice with my band, Banned.

9:00 p.m.: I walk back to the liquor store and purchase another twelve-pack of Budweiser.

9:15 p.m.: Two girls come into the studio with a case of wine coolers. I think to myself that I hate wine coolers but would drink them if I ran out of beer, which I always did.

9:20 p.m.: We continue practicing as the girls watch us.

9:30 p.m.: Two more girls come into the studio with a bottle of Yukon Jack. I thought that Yukon tastes like cough syrup, but what the hell. There are now four girls in the studio, and three of them were hot.

10:00 p.m.: We finish practice, drink the rest of the beer, wine coolers, and Yukon Jack.

10:20 p.m.: We start breaking down our equipment and loading everything into our vehicles.

10:30 p.m.: The first two hot girls leave. The other two girls stay to help us get our equipment home.

10:34 p.m.: The one hot girl hits on my singer. The other girl is a nasty-looking woodland creature–like girl with matted brown hair and freckles. My drummer sees this and jumps in the car with the singer and the hot girl leaving me stuck with the rat-girl who is obviously interested in hooking up with me.

10:52 p.m.: Me and Rat-girl get to my house, and I unload my equipment leaving her in the car. I grab an eighth of weed and some beer.

11:00 p.m.: We head to the hot girl's house off Brookhurst Street in Fountain Valley. I meet up with everyone else there to continue partying.

11:25 p.m.: I get pulled over by a Fountain Valley squad car right in front of the hot girl's house. Rat-girl gives me a piece of gum. Now remember I had already drank a case of Budweiser, a case of wine coolers, and a fifth of Yukon Jack. I tell him that I was taking Rat-girl home and that she just lived across the street. He asks me if I had been drinking, and I tell him no. He knows I was lying to him but agreed to let me go if I stay parked and walk across the street to her house. CLOSE CALL!

11:45 p.m.: Me and Rat-girl finally get to the hot girl's house. I explain to the guys what had just happened to me and that I needed a beer.

11:50 p.m.: The five of us drink and smoke.

12:45 a.m.: My singer and the hot girl start making out on the couch and decide to go upstairs and hook up.

12:46 a.m.: Rat-girl takes this as her cue and starts hitting on me.

12:47 a.m.: I am very drunk and stoned. I laugh at her and tell her that even if she were the last woman on earth and the future of mankind depended on us procreating to further our race, that I would not fuck her and our species would die out.

12:48 a.m.: Rat-girl gets offended by what I said and scratches me on the arm with her little claws and calls me a pig. Really? Who scratches someone like an animal like that? A slap across the face or a kick in the balls I would have understood, but *scratching* someone? Well, I guess there's a first time for everything.

12:49 a.m.: I am still laughing at her and making pig noises through my nose while my arm bleeds through my shirt sleeve.

12:50 a.m.: Rat-girl starts crying and runs upstairs. Too much Yukon Jack, I guess?

12:51 a.m.: I look at my drummer and shrug my shoulders. We sit on the rug in front of the coffee table, and I roll a joint.

1:10 a.m.: We are stoned, and we discuss the events of the evening.

1:30 a.m.: We decide to leave and go home.

1:31 a.m.: As we are leaving, Rat-girl's boyfriend—yes, she has a boyfriend—runs past us up the driveway to go console and fuck that troubled little ugly girl.

1:36 a.m.: We get in the car and pull out onto Brookhurst Street.

1:57 a.m.: We drive for a little while, and I get pulled over again. Fuck! I am even more drunk and stoned than the first time I got pulled over.

1:58 a.m.: I pull over into the parking lot of a Denny's.

2:04 a.m.: The cop asks me if I had been drinking, and instead of lying like I did before, I say yes. Big mistake. (NEVER admit that you have been drinking to a cop! Ever!) That was it; I had pushed it. Tempted fate too much. The gods were frowning upon me for mocking them and driving again after they had let me get away with it earlier that night. I fail the field sobriety tests miserably and get seated in the back of his squad car.

2:22 a.m.: I am taken away to jail, and my drummer, who is too drunk to drive himself, is left to fend for himself. I later learn that he actually got a ride all the way home from an old man who was in Denny's watching the whole thing through the window of the restaurant as he ate. So he didn't have to walk. Not bad for him.

2:43 a.m.: I am booked and fingerprinted. The cop who arrests me look like he was Hawaiian, and as he searches me, he finds pot in my pocket. He comments that it looks like very good pot, which it is. I tell him that if he lets me go, he can have it. He laughs but doesn't let me go. I know that son of a bitch kept it anyway because there was no mention of it in my police report.

3:00 a.m.: They take my blood to see how drunk I was and put me in a cell with only a cot in it.

3:45 a.m.: The Hawaiian cop that stole my weed comes back to tell me how impressed he was that my BAC (blood alcohol content) was .29, and I was still functioning. The legal driving limit in California was .08. I was more than three times the legal limit. He goes on to say that at .30, you slip into a coma. I told him, "Only if you're a fuckin' pussy."

3:46 a.m.: He leaves me alone. I just sit there and do not sleep at all.

7:30 a.m.: I am released from jail.

7:31 a.m.: I walk three miles down Brookhurst Street till I spot a payphone.

8:15 a.m.: I call a friend to come pick me up.

8:16 a.m.: I start walking again.

9:05 a.m.: My friend picks me up and takes me home.

9:30 a.m.: I finally get home and go to bed immediately. It is now April 13, 1989.

Past Lives

Johnny was an amateur hypnotist. He learned the basics at a local community college. His mother was paying for the classes, and they lived together in a small house in the valley. Johnny always had visions of grandeur. When he was little, he pictured himself as a famous magician like Harry Houdini stunning the crowds making them awe in amazement.

Unfortunately, he wasn't very good at it. Maybe he could make it as a hypnotist. One Friday night, they were watching television, and a show came on about reincarnation. There was a guy that would "transgress" people back in time to past lives using hypnosis. They told stories about their old jobs, whether they were male or female, if they had kids, things like that. This amazed Johnny!

"That's what I want to do, Mom! I want to take people back in time!" he said loudly.

"But that's simply not real, Johnny. Those people are just actors."

"No, it is. They were talking about it in my class. That's the real deal, and I'll prove it to you!"

"How are you going to do that? You don't even have your license yet," she said.

"I'll show you how to hypnotize me, and you will see that I have past lives!"

"Impossible."

They went into the backroom where he had a chair and a couch set up. He would practice there at night, but this time it was for real.

"Sit there, Mom, and I'll lay down here."

He very basically taught her how to put him under. Most importantly, he showed her how to bring him back.

"Make sure I can hear your voice CLEARLY then count backwards from 3, 2, 1, then snap your fingers, and I will wake up. It's that easy," he said.

His mother followed his directions and successfully put him under surprisingly easy. She instructed him to go back to his first life. He told her that it was the year 1206. He was a woman named Mary who was banished from her tribe because she couldn't have children. He was very upset and started speaking in Arabic. His mother couldn't believe it! She knew that her son didn't speak any other languages. It was too much for her to take. Her heart raced pounding in her chest. She fell to her knees grabbing her cell phone; she dialed 911 and collapsed to the floor.

Johnny's journey continued into a new life. It was now the 1500s, and he was a knight fighting for King Henry against the French, as the paramedics broke down the front door of their house. Then he was an 1800s slave trafficker transporting Negroes from Africa to the New World, as the paramedics drove them both through the streets to the hospital. Next, he was in the 1900s Depression Era working as the manager of a factory when they finally reached the hospital. His mom lay dead on her stretcher from a massive heart attack. Johnny was motionless from what they thought was a coma. All his vitals were good; he just wouldn't wake up. They didn't realize he was under hypnosis. When he got to his current life, he saw himself laying on a table under a light. His mother was standing next to him.

"You were right, son. You had many past lives. I'm going to my next one. I'll see you on the other side, my love."

Realizing he's still under hypnosis, he wonders without his mom alive; how will he ever snap out of it? His mother just strolled down the hallway with a big smile. Into the light, and her next life.

She Said

"You need to get a new fucking bed!" she said out of nowhere.

"Why, what's wrong with the one I have?" I said very confused.

"Only God knows how many sluts have slept with you in that one."

"Well, you didn't have a problem with it last night."

"Well, I have a problem with it now."

"Sleep on the floor then."

"What, do you think I'm your dog?"

"What the hell? Why are you tripping out? Did I do something wrong?"

"Yeah, you slept with a bunch of whores in that bed."

"Go sleep on the couch then, you fucking weirdo!"

She ripped the comforter off my tainted bed and stormed down the hallway into the living room. I have no idea what set her off. Apparently she just snapped. I turned out the light and got into bed. She only left me the sheet, so I covered up the best I could. I laid there wondering what I had done to deserve such treatment. Eventually I fell asleep. The next morning, I woke up and she was laying beside me. Her back was to me, and she was snoring. Her bare skin looked beautiful in the morning sunlight. Just another small victory in this war I call life.

The Nirvana Dildo

We were in my friend Matt's garage drinking beer and getting high. There were four of us. Matt, Derrick, Moe, and myself. It was a preshow ritual that we had been doing for years. That night, we were going to see the band Nirvana. Derrick had just been kicked out of his girlfriend's apartment that day for cheating on her. He had a big duffel bag with all his stuff in it.

"Fuck that bitch!" he said angrily.

"Here, take a bong toke. It'll make you feel better," I said.

"Well, it is kind of your fault, dude. After all, you did cheat on her," Moe said with a smirk.

"Yeah, and the chick that you cheated on with her was fat! What were you thinking?" Matt said laughing.

We all started laughing except for Derrick. He was just looking down at the floor.

"I was drunk. I dunno. It just happened. I don't really remember." He was still looking down.

"Well, there's nothing you can do about it now. What's done is done. Let's just finish these beers, get really high, and go have fun at the

Nirvana show! After the show, you can stay at my place until you can figure out where to go," I preached.

Everyone nodded in agreement. We all cracked open a new beer and did a Cheers. I was packing another round in the bong when Derrick unzipped his bag and reached inside. He pulled out a big dark purple dildo and shoved it in my face.

"What the fuck are you doing, man? What is that thing?" I screamed.

"It's that bitch's dildo," he said triumphantly.

"Well, now you're not getting another bong toke. How do you like that?" I was disgusted as I passed the bong to Matt.

"What did you do, steal it from her?" Matt said in between hits.

"Yeah, man. When she was throwing all my shit out into the living room, I reached into the nightstand by the bed and took it. Now she won't be having no fun tonight!" He was very pleased with himself.

"Well, if you stick that thing in my face again, you'll be going to the fucking hospital, not a Nirvana show." I was serious.

Everybody started laughing except me, of course.

"All right, you homos, let's get going or we're gonna be late."

We got everything together and piled into Moe's car. Moe was driving, Matt was shotgun, I was behind Moe in the backseat, and in between Derrick and I was his bag of shit. The first thing we did was go straight to the liquor store and buy more beer. Then we hit the road. Of course, living in Southern California, we got stuck in traffic. So I cracked open a beer, Moe turned up the stereo, and we tried to make the best of it. I looked out the window to my left and noticed two pretty girls in the car next to us. I did a little hand gesture to get the attention of the girl on the passenger side, and it worked. She looked over. I held up my beer and pointed to it to see if they wanted to party. She turned and said something to her friend, and then they both looked over and started giggling. I elbowed Derrick.

"Dude, check out these chicks."

I lifted my hands like I was awaiting their answer. The passenger pointed at her watch as if to say they didn't have time. Derrick would have none of that and unzipped his bag. He pulled out the dildo and started waving it in the air. The only word that I can use to describe the look on their faces is *horror*! These were young girls, not street whores. He started motioning like he was jerking it off and rolling his eyes back in his head. At this point I was cracking up. I'm sorry, but he looked like some kind of spastic, hairless chimpanzee jerking off. He was obviously still pissed at his ex-girlfriend and taking it out on these poor young women.

"What are you guys doing back there?" Moe said.

"Shut up and drive!" we both said at the exact same time.

The girls turned to their left into the carpool lane to escape Derrick's torment. That lane was moving faster, and off they went away from Derrick's abuse.

"That was fun. Now it's your turn," he said with a twinkle in his eye.

"You're a sick motherfucker, you know that, right?"

"Yes," he said proudly.

He passed me the dildo like it was a baton in the fucking Olympic Games. After all, it was pretty funny, traffic was boring, and we were high and drunk.

"Okay, let's see who comes up next."

The next car was a work truck with two Mexicans in it. I unzipped my zipper and put the bottom of the dildo in my pants. Derrick just smiled. I put my face close to the glass and waved at the man in the passenger seat. He turned to his right and looked at me. I gave him a kind of retarded face and crossed my eyes. He nudged the driver with his left elbow, and they both just looked at me. At this time, traffic had stopped so we were right next to each other. I tilted my head back and arched my back. Slowly I raised my pelvis to reveal the big purple dildo in all its splendor. The Mexicans just watched in amazement at what they were witnessing. Derrick started acting like a monkey again and was worshiping my appendage vigorously. Now Moe and Matt had figured out what we were doing and were almost crying from laughter in the front seats. I slowly started to gyrate my hips like Elvis used to do. Then suddenly I thrust my midsection up and down violently bending the dildo to and fro. This excited monkey Derrick greatly, and he began smacking it with his hand. I looked out of the corner of my left eye, and the two guys burst out in laughter! They had realized we were just fucking with them, and to their credit, had a very sick sense of humor. They did the same as the girl and turned left into the fast lane and got out of there. Imagine the story that they would tell their friends and family when they got home. Now remember, all four of us are drunk and high and now smell blood in the water.

"Do it again, dude," Matt said wiping a tear from his eye.

"Yeah, who's next?" Moe added.

"Okay, okay, hold your horses, guys," I said.

The next car to pull next to us was a middle-aged couple. The man was driving.

"I don't know, guys. They look kind of old."

They all urged me to go for it. I did the same as before, making a face through the window, but she must have thought I was really retarded because she just gave me this sweet smile. I tilted back my head and arched my back and raised myself. In an instant, her smile turned to pure disgust. She said something to her husband, and he started yelling at me. It looked like she had a cell phone in her hand.

"Abort the mission, abort the mission! Moe, get us the fuck outta here!" I screamed.

Of course, as most hoodlums do, we had taken it too far. Moe found some space to the right and got away from them. They were still somewhere behind us but caught in traffic.

"Whew, that was a close one!" Moe sighed.

"Here, take this goddamn thing and put it back in your bag. Fucking monkey boy." My heart was still racing.

Derrick put it back in his bag, and everything went back to normal.

A few minutes later, we were at a standstill stuck in traffic, and there was a tap on Moe's window. It was a motorcycle cop that had caught up to us by maneuvering between the cars. Moe rolled his window down.

"I'm going to need you to pull over, son." The cop did not look happy.

"What's the problem, officer?" Moe asked.

"Just pull over. Now."

Moe changed lanes and started toward the off ramp with the cop following behind us lights flashing. It was still daytime, but all eyes were on us. This was the conversation in the car at that moment.

"Thanks a lot, Jack. Another fine mess you've gotten us into!" Moe said angrily.

"What are you talking about? You're the one that told me to do it again!" I said in defense.

"Now we're going to miss the show." Matt put his hands over his face.

"Fuck the show! We're all going to jail!"

"Well, me and Matt didn't do anything. It was all you two," Moe yelled.

"If you want to blame someone, blame monkey boy over here. It's his goddamn dildo!" I yelled back.

"It's not my dildo! I told you it's my girlfriend's dildo!"

"Ex-girlfriend!" we all yelled at the same time.

"By the way, dude, what was up with the all that monkey shit? That was kind of weird," I whispered to him.

"I was acting like one of those flying monkeys from *The Wizard of Oz.*"

"But they have wings. You don't have wings. So how do you think the people in the other car would know if you were a flying monkey or a regular monkey?"

"I dunno." He really didn't know.

"Hello! Toto and Dorothy. We have a fucking cop behind us! What are we going to do?" Moe was starting to freak out.

We were now hitting the off ramp and getting off the freeway. I knew I had to take charge of these idiots, and fast.

"Okay, here's the plan. Everyone down their beers!"

"You're the only one with a beer!" They all yelled back.

I downed my beer.

"Okay, who has the weed?"

"You have the weed!" They all yelled back again.

Fuck, this was going to be harder than I thought. Maybe I was the idiot. I had some beautiful fluffy Northern California skunk buds with orange hairs. I took the baggy and smashed them down into the side of my boot.

"Pull into this grocery store parking lot. That way, if we get arrested, they won't impound your car."

"I better not get arrested. I didn't do anything!" Now Moe was really freaking out.

We pulled over on the side of the store by a dumpster, and Moe rolled down his window.

"License and registration, please." The cop's face was stern.

"What's the problem, officer?"

"A woman called 911 and said that a retarded man in a blue Volvo showed her his penis on the freeway."

"Well, I can assure you officer that it wasn't me."

"She also said that it was the person in the backseat behind the driver." He looked right at me.

"You. Get out of the car."

I got out of the car.

"Did you show your penis to a woman on the freeway earlier today?"

"No, sir, I certainly did not," I said because I fucking didn't!

"Where are you guys heading?"

"To go see a band called Nirvana, sir."

"I've heard that they are good. Are they?"

"Yeah, well, I guess. Yeah, they're pretty good." What the hell was going on here?

"Do you want to make it to the concert tonight?"

"Yes, sir."

"Then stop lying to me and tell me what the hell is going on here!" he yelled right in my face.

"Okay, well, Derrick's ex-girlfriend kicked him out of her house, so now he's homeless, and out of spite, he stole her dildo and put it in his bag, and he brought his bag with us, and then he pulled it out and acted like a flying monkey and started jerking it off in front of these girls, and they freaked out and called 911 on him."

"That's not true, officer!" Derrick yelled.

"All right, then you tell me what happened then?" He put his right arm on the roof of the car and leaned down.

"Well, first of all, she's still my girlfriend, and second of all, I'm not homeless. It all started when Jack unzipped his pants and put the dildo in his zipper then he showed it to the Mexicans and the old lady."

"What Mexicans? What dildo? Did you show a dildo to some Mexican's son?" He looked at me.

I just looked down and didn't answer. I was ashamed. He walked over to his motorcycle and opened the side compartment and pulled out a rubber glove.

"Where's this dildo now?" he asked me.

"It's in his bag, sir." I pointed at Derrick

"Let me have it." He held out his hand.

Derrick opened the bag and gave the big purple dildo to the cop.

"So all this was a joke? None of you kids showed your penises to anybody?"

We all looked down and shook our heads no.

"I wish my dick was that big," Derrick said out of nowhere.

"One more word out of you and I'll take you to jail just because I don't like you," he shouted.

Derrick never spoke again.

"Do you have any illegal drugs in the car with you?"

"No, sir." Technically I wasn't lying because the pot was in my boot, and I wasn't in the car.

"How about anything else?"

"Just some beer."

He walked over to the dumpster and threw the dildo away. As he turned, I caught a glimpse of a faint smile on his face. He walked back.

"Let me see the beer."

I leaned down and gave him the twelve-pack of beer.

"It's open and one is missing. Where did it go?"

"I drank it back at the house," I said.

"Well, I can't let you go with an open box of beer, so you have a choice. Pour out this beer or you all go to jail."

I grabbed the twelver, went over to the dumpster, and one by one poured out each bottle and threw them in the trash.

"I'm going to let you all go with a warning. If I see you again today, I'm going to take you all to jail for indecent exposure. Now get out of here!"

I walked back to the car and got in. Moe started it up, and we got out of there and drove directly back to the freeway. The cop followed us. Probably to make sure we didn't stop for more beer. When we got to the on ramp, he veered off to the left and took off. As we were driving down the freeway, Derrick spoke.

"That motherfucker threw my girlfriend's dildo away!"

"Ex-girlfriend!" we all said together.

Moe turned the stereo up, and not much was said after that. Nirvana actually put on a really good show that night. I still have the ticket stub to this day.

The Foul-Mouthed Macaw

When I was dating my daughter's mother, she lived out in Ontario, California. The people who lived directly behind her house had a parrot. I believe it was a macaw. It was a huge, colorful bird, with a very loud voice. Now Ontario is in the 909 area code. If you live in Southern California, you know what that means. So instead of teaching this beautiful animal to sing songs or recite limericks, they thought it would be a smart idea to teach it profanity. You could hear it scream at the top of its lungs, "Fuck you, asshole" or "Eat shit and die" or "Suck my cock" at any time during the day or night. Especially late at night. At the time, I thought it was annoying being insulted every day and night with these obscenities. This morning, I was thinking about that bird, and today I actually miss him. I read that macaws can live to be over fifty years old. So maybe he could still be out there in the 909 screaming away, "Eat my fuck, asshole" in all his majestic glory!

Alien Arrest

House arrest, shit! I'm sitting here in the middle of the day on house arrest as sentenced by the Orange County courthouse for a DUI. Well, I guess it's better than being in jail. The great Texas band Butthole Surfers have a song called "Alcohol," and the only words in the song are "Alcohol, you son of a bitch" over and over again. Maybe they were on to something. So my attorney got me house arrest instead of 240 days in the O.C. jail. It wasn't cheap, but who can put a price on freedom? I had to go to this little office in Santa Ana called Sentinel. I met with a skinny Mexican guy with a bad attitude. Probably pissed off because he couldn't make it as a cop and had to settle for working for a probation company. He went over all the rules, like I can't leave my apartment at any time for any reason unless approved by him or one of the other angry Mexicans who worked there. Not even to step outside for a smoke. He told me I had to blow the smoke out through the window. I could go to work from 6:00 a.m. to 6:00 p.m., not a minute before, or a minute after, or VIOLATION! I could go to the grocery store on Saturday from 1:00 p.m. to 3:00 p.m., not a minute before, or a minute after or VIOLATION! I could go to church on Sunday from 10:00 a.m. to 1:00 p.m., not a minute before, well, you get it. Or VIOLATION! He took me into a room with a big black box on a table. The box had a small circular hole in the center of it and what looked to be some sort of small TV screen sticking out of the top. He put a straw into the hole.

"This is your breathalyzer. It will tell us if you've drank any alcohol when you are at home. When it beeps, I want you to push the start button, and then I want you to blow into the straw as hard as you can until it beeps again," he said.

The box beeped and I blew. After about three seconds, it beeped again and FLASH, it took my fuckin' picture! *Wow*, I thought, *pretty high-tech!* No getting around this thing. Then he took me into the restroom and told me to piss into a cup. He watched me as I pissed into the cup, and I felt a little weird. I think he enjoyed it a lot more than I did. Next, we went into another room where he had me sit in a chair. He told me to take off my left shoe and sock. He put this rubber anklet around my ankle and locked it into place.

"Do not tamper with the ankle bracelet at all or you'll get a violation," he said. I was starting to sense a theme here.

"You'll get used to it after a few days."

He left the room and came back with a black phonelike thing about as big as a small brick and what looked like a phone charger.

"This is your GPS tracking unit. When you leave your house, your ankle bracelet will let us know the minute you leave your front door. You are to carry this GPS unit in your pocket at all times when you're outside your house so we can track your whereabouts. Any unapproved locations you go to will be a violation. The minute you get home, you are to put the tracking device back into this charger. If you let the tracking device go dead, it will be a violation. Got it?"

"Got it," I said.

I got the breathalyzer, GPS unit, and charger together, filled out some more forms, paid them some money, and got the hell out of there. By the time I got home, it was early Friday evening. I set all the equipment up and sat in my chair. *Only 239 more days of this shit to go*, I thought to myself.

So it started out slow. I would stand by the window when I smoked cigarettes and blow the smoke out the window. Then I stood at the threshold of my front door to smoke. One day I stuck my leg out so my ankle bracelet was outside my door. Nothing happened. I walked out to the sidewalk, then ran back in. Still nothing. I felt foolish, but nothing happened. I had a landline telephone that had to be open at all times. If I did something to violate my house arrest, or get in trouble in any way, my probation officer or one of his cronies would call, but the phone didn't ring. The next morning was Saturday. I walked out to the dumpster behind my apartment and dumped my trash and ran back. The phone didn't ring. Then I walked over to my mailbox and got my mail. I could see that as long as I stayed pretty close to the apartment, I would be okay. I went to work the next week and continued to figure out what I could and couldn't do, but I never really pushed it. I didn't want to go back to jail; they had the wrong kind of bars in there.

I was about seven months into my sentence, Thursday, March 3, to be exact, and I was very tired. It had been a long work week, and I still had one day to go, so I went to bed early, but I couldn't sleep. I tossed and turned for a while then turned on the TV. The last thing I remember was the *Late, Late Show* being on, which ends at 1:37 a.m. I turned off the TV and finally fell asleep. I began to feel a heavy pressure on my chest, and my hands felt very light, like two balloons. My head hurt too. Like a migraine, but I hadn't had headaches like that since I was a kid. I had a dream, and in it was this dark figure. He was skinny and moved VERY fast. I could never get a good look at him. Just out of the corner of my eye, and then I would turn and he was gone. I got a very negative feeling from him. This guy was not good at all!

I awoke the next morning to my landline ringing. I jumped out of bed and ran over to the phone.

"Hello?" I said

"This is Officer Valdez of the Orange County Probation Department. Is this Jack Bell?" he said in a stern voice.

"Yes, this is Jack."

"Our records show that at 3:33 a.m. last night you left your residence. Where did you go?"

"I'm sorry, sir, but I can assure you I have been home all night! I was just getting up for work. There must be some mistake," I said in a confused tone.

"Are you sure you didn't leave AT ALL last night?"

"Positive. I was asleep in bed all night."

"Well, my computer shows that your GPS device detected that your ankle bracelet was out of range from it at 3:33 a.m. and stays like that for an hour, till 4:33 a.m. Didn't you hear it ringing?"

"No, I didn't hear anything."

"Well, the strange thing is that your ankle bracelet doesn't show that you left, just that you were too far away from the GPS. There must be a malfunction in the equipment. You must bring everything down to the department for inspection. Any tampering with that equipment will put you in direct violation of your probation!"

"I understand that, officer, but I swear I didn't tamper with anything."

"You need to bring everything to me right now!" he barked.

"It's Friday. Can I bring it by after work?"

"No, you must bring it over now."

I unplugged all the equipment, called my office to let them know that I wouldn't be in, and went to the probation department in Santa Ana. When I got there, Officer Valdez was waiting for me.

"My technician is going to inspect this equipment, and if there is any evidence of tampering, you will go directly to jail," he said as he pointed to a police car outside the window.

"I didn't touch anything," I said with my hands in the air.

"Sit down in that chair so I can keep an eye on you."

I sat down. His technician took the equipment into the other room. Officer Valdez just sat behind his desk and stared at me.

"I've been doing this for a long time, Mr. Bell, and 99% of the time this happens, my equipment has been tampered with. Joe will figure out what you did. You guys never learn. You can't outsmart the law."

I just sat there. I knew from experience NEVER to speak in situations like this with the cops. ANYTHING you say could be construed any way they wanted. I really didn't know what happened last night though. I never touched any of that equipment, and it had been working fine for seven months.

Joe was gone about half an hour. He came out of the room looking puzzled.

"Nothing wrong with it, boss," Joe said sounding afraid.

"What do you mean?"

"I gave it a thorough checkout. It works fine."

Officer Valdez looked at me.

"I told you! Guess I'm the 1%, huh?" I said. I know I shouldn't have, but the asshole in me couldn't resist.

"Give him back the damn thing," Officer Valdez said with disgust.

"I want you to follow him back to his apartment and set it up yourself," he told Joe.

I got the damn thing and got out of there. Joe followed me back to my apartment. When we got there, Joe started setting up everything again.

"I swear Joe, I didn't touch any of this shit yesterday," I said.

"Don't worry about it. I'll make sure it's set up right this time."

"But it's been here for seven months already, and I never had a problem before. Now Valdez has a hard-on for me!"

"He's just pissed off because he never made it as a cop, so he takes it out on you guys. Don't worry, I'll take care of you if anything else happens."

I could tell Joe was a good guy, but I was still nervous about Valdez. I still had a few weeks of this shit to go. Till March 25. Joe left, and I sat there wondering what happened. I remembered feeling weird before I fell asleep and then that scary dream of the dark figure. He moved so fast. Very strange.

It was Friday night, so I was glad that I didn't have to work the next day. That night I was in bed watching the *Late, Late Show* again and began to fall asleep, so I turned the TV off. As I fell asleep, I began feeling that pressure on my chest and my hands felt like balloons again. My head began to ache just like when I was a kid. All of a sudden, there was a bright white light in my room that blinded me. I was scared and confused. I saw that dark figure in the corner of my room flashing in and out of the light. He told me not to be afraid, that he wasn't going to hurt me, but he didn't move his mouth. He was somehow talking in my head. I remember trying to talk back, but I couldn't. He told me that he needed me because I was special. I was a number 9. He needed a number 9?

I woke up to the landline ringing. I looked at the clock; it was 4:33 a.m. I got up and tried to run into the living room to get it, but my back hurt, and I had a terrible headache. I got to the phone and answered it.

"Hello."

"Hello, Jack. This is Joe."

"What's the matter, Joe?"

"Your GPS has been blowing up over here! I've been calling you for an hour. Where the hell have you been?"

"I've been here, Joe, I swear!"

"Well, your ankle bracelet shows you've been there, but the GPS shows you were too far away from it. Why didn't you answer the phone?"

"I must have been sleeping."

"You're lucky Valdez is off on Friday night or he'd be shitting a Twinkie over this! I don't know what you're doing over there, but you'd better stop. I'll cover for you this time. Don't let it happen again."

I thanked Joe and hung up the phone. What the hell *was* going on with me? I felt like I had a hangover, but I hadn't drunk in six months? All I could remember was the number 9. Over and over in my head, 9, 9, 9.

It was Saturday morning, and I checked all the equipment. Everything seems okay. While I was in the shower, I got an idea. I would stay up all night to try and find out what the hell was going on. When I got out of the shower. I called my friend Daryl. Daryl was a coke dealer, and I figured that would help me stay up to figure this out. I picked up the phone and dialed.

"Daryl, this is Jack."

"Wassup, my man?" he said.

"You got any blow?"

"Ya, but you don't do blow Jack. You havin' a party tonight?"

"It's for a chick I got comin' over, she's into that," I said off the top of my head.

"Ahhh, gotcha. Aren't you on house arrest, though?"

"Ya, but they only check me for alcohol, not drugs. Can you bring it over?"

"No worries, my man. Be there in half an hour."

Daryl came by with the coke, and we both did a line.

"Well, I better get outta here before that chick gets here," he said.

"Ya, thanks, man. I owe you one."

Daryl left. I couldn't tell him why I wanted the blow. He would have thought I was crazy. Maybe I was.

That night I was halfway through the bindle he had brought me and wide awake. I hated coke because it made me paranoid, but I had to stay awake somehow. I sat in my reclining chair in the living room thinking about that dark figure. What had he meant about me being a number 9?

It was early in the morning, about 3:30 a.m., when my TV started to get all fuzzy. Then it turned to static snow. I was wide awake this time. I started to feel the pressure on my chest, and my hands began to rise from my chair. The lights went off, and a bright white light filled my living room. Oh shit, it's happening again, and this time I'm awake! The dark figure appeared in the corner of the room and began talking to me in my head again. He told me not to be afraid, that he wouldn't hurt me. My balloon hands began to lift me into the light. I rose from my chair and went right through the ceiling. As I went up, I could hear my GPS unit start ringing. The sound got farther and farther away as I ascended. When the light died down, I was in a room on a hard, cold table. The dark figure was there with a few of his buddies. They were standing in the shadows, so I couldn't really see them, but I knew it was him, and he was bad. I couldn't talk, but he knew what I was thinking. I told him that I had an ankle bracelet on and that the police would come looking for me, so he'd better let me go. He said to me telepathically that he had time and would try to explain everything to me since I was awake this time. He said he was from far away and wanted to help the human race. They needed tissue samples of DNA for their project. He said that the universe was all about numbers and numerology and mathematics, and I couldn't comprehend what they needed to do. He said that he could only get to me at 3:33 a.m. because that was the symbol of the Father, the Son, and the Holy Ghost. The trilogy of three. I didn't feel he was holy, though. He could only take me for three nights as he did thirty-three years ago when I was a child. This was also how old Jesus was when he died, thirty-three. That is why I remembered the chest pressure, balloon hands, and the headaches when I was a kid. He said the headaches were from the altitude that we were at, but I would be fine. I remember thinking if he was such an intellectual being, why didn't he grab my GPS unit, forgetting that they could read my mind. He didn't like that and explained that they didn't want to be tracked. I thought even telepathically I could be an asshole. He didn't respond. He told me that centuries ago they were attracted to the beautiful women of Earth and came down and had sex with them. Sometimes the offspring would be great rulers or demigods, but sometimes, it didn't turn out so good. He talked of cyclopses, centaurs, and giants as also being their offspring. He said that God didn't like this and would kill these beings on Earth. He used the example of David and Goliath. Goliath was a nine-foot-tall giant, or Nephilim as the Bible calls them, and one of their offspring. God helped David slay the giant with a simple slingshot. So then they started tinkering with DNA thinking that if their offspring would look just like us, God wouldn't know who was theirs and who was his. We'd all look alike. They wanted to make a supreme human that looked exactly like us, with the powers of a god, to rule over Earth. They had come close twice before but had failed. He put pictures of Napoleon and Hitler in my head. *These fuckers are talking about the anti-Christ*, I thought. He didn't deny my thought. He said they were sure they'd get it right the *third* time He said that they had chosen me as a child for my DNA but had to wait till I was an adult to come back for me on March 3. 3/3 for 3 days. It was starting to make sense now. 3—3—3. That's why they got me at 3:33 a.m. on March 3. I asked him why he had called me number 9? He said it was because 3 + 3 + 3 = 9 and because of numerology. In Chinese numerology, they believe that every human has nine lives, like the stories you hear of cats when you're a kid, but it's true. People in their ninth life have the most life experience, so they're the special souls that they needed. My birthday is April 17, 1968. 0 + 4 + 1 + 7 + 1 + 9 + 6 + 8 = 36. Broken down to single digits is 3 + 6 = 9. Number 9. After I die, this time I won't be reincarnated; I will either go to heaven or hell. He was right; I was getting overwhelmed with all this information and numbers and shit. Then he said that he was disappointed in me that I'd snorted the cocaine to stay awake. He needed me to be asleep to do the DNA sampling, and since I did the drug, my body was tainted unlike when I was a child. So after all that, he couldn't use me. He said his time was up and that I wouldn't remember any of this when I woke up. He apologized that he had to get me back to my apartment before the police arrived. *What*, I thought, *the police?*

I awoke to my landline ringing and the cops pounding on my door. I let them in, and they pushed me to the ground and handcuffed me behind my back. They asked me where I had been. I couldn't remember. I didn't say a word. It was Sunday morning, and they took me to jail. I did my remaining nineteen days in Orange County Jail and got out at 7:00 p.m. on March 25. I got home and laid on my bed. After all those days, I still couldn't remember what I'd done, where I'd gone, or what had happened. The sheriffs even smacked me around a little bit in there trying to get it out of me, but I had nothing. When they realized it, they finally left me alone. It was good to be back home and in my own bed, though. It was Friday night. I watched the *Late, Late Show* and then fell asleep. I woke up in the morning and had a big stretch and yawn. It looked like a nice sunny day outside. I got out of bed and walked into my living room. My laptop computer was in front of my chair and open. I thought that was strange because I hadn't used my computer the night before. I sat down and looked at the monitor. I couldn't believe what I was seeing! This story was written on it.

Thor's Hammer

Purple like the mountains

Purple like the smog

Purple like an iris

Purple like my rock-hard cock

Veneration

"Veneration," she said.

"Veneration for your cock."

"I want to worship it."

"I want to worship it like a Greek god!"

"Like Thor's hammer!"

"But alas, I am on my period."

"God has punished women with this affliction."

"Every month that we do not conceive." She sighed and looked down.

"Well, your asshole's not on its period," I said.

"You know that hurts me too much. I do not like it." She shook her head.

"But I'll tell you what."

"I'll suck Thor's hammer until its lightning bolt blows the back of my fucking head out!"

"That's okay, honey." I gently moved her hair out of her face.

"Why don't we just drink some beer and watch television?"

Millionaire in One Day

It was a rough morning. I had stayed up late the night before drinking. It was time to pull myself together and go out and find a job, but first, I needed some coffee. I drove down to the corner coffee shop to get a cup and a donut. As I pulled into the parking lot, I noticed a red Ferrari parked right in the front. When I got inside, I saw my old friend from high school, Scott. He looked great. Nice fresh haircut and an expensive suit and shoes. I got in line. After he paid for his coffee, he turned around and saw me. I hadn't had a haircut in a while and was definitely not wearing a suit.

"Jack, is that you?" he said with a smile.

"Hey there, Scotty. How's it going?"

"Awesome, man! How about yourself?"

"I'm okay, just a little slow from last night so I thought I'd grab a quick cup of coffee."

"I hear ya. So where you working at now?" he said.

"At the moment, I'm unemployed." I felt ashamed.

"Got any kids?" he asked.

"I have a teenage daughter, but I'm not married, so it's just me and her. How about you?"

"I have a son, but he had to go away for a while."

"Sorry to hear that."

"Well, I just started at this place a week ago, and I'm doing awesome!"

"Good for you." I think he sensed disdain in my voice.

"Come with me. I want to show you something."

We walked outside and went over to the Ferrari.

"This is my new car. I just bought it yesterday," he said proudly.

"Wow, that's beautiful. I noticed it right when I pulled in the parking lot, but I thought you only started at your job a week ago?"

"I did."

"And you bought this car yesterday?"

"Yep, and I paid cash."

"So how does that work?"

"How would you like to be a millionaire in one day?" he said.

"Come on, dude, don't fuck with me. I just told you I don't have a job. You don't have to rub it in."

"No, seriously. Get in your truck and follow me to my work. I'll see if I can get you a job."

I got in my truck and followed him thinking he's full of shit. We drove on the freeway for a while and got off by this warehouse. We parked and Scott came over.

"This is it," he said.

"This is what?"

"This is where I work."

The building didn't look like much, but there were millions of dollars' worth of sports cars, hot rods, and monster trucks outside.

"So you work for a car dealership?" I said.

"Come inside and check it out." He laughed.

He opened the door and we went in. It was a huge warehouse. There were a bunch of guys sitting at desks talking on telephones.

"Let me go talk to my boss and let him know that you're a single dad looking for a job."

He walked into an office. I stood there listening to the men on the phones. Some of them were talking different languages. At the far end of the room was a woman sitting in what looked to be a large trade desk with a counter in front of it. After a few minutes, Scotty came out of the office with a big smile.

"Okay, the boss says to give you a shot. Sit here at this desk."

I sat down.

"All you have to do is sign these contracts, and you're in."

I looked over the papers, and it all seemed legit. I signed the contracts.

"I personally guarantee this lead is a home run. Just tell him you're calling from this company, read this pitch, and at the end, ask the guy if he wants to buy five hundred thousand shares of this stock. Now go ahead and dial it," he said.

"Are you shitting me, man?"

"I shit you not. Now call him!"

I dialed the number and spoke with a man who agreed to buy five hundred thousand shares of the stock. I was amazed!

"See, I told you it was guaranteed! You just made $100,000, buddy! Now do you think you can do that ten times today?" he asked.

"Fuck ya I can. Are you kidding me!" I screamed.

"If you can, you will be a millionaire by the time the sun goes down tonight!"

"Okay, so what do I do now?" I inquired.

"Just take that ticket over to the trade desk, and Linda will give you a check."

"Who's Linda?"

She's the boss's wife. She runs the trade desk and hands out the checks after a sale."

I ran over to the trade desk. I told Linda my name, and that this was my first sale. She smiled back at me with an evil glare.

"Congratulations! Now you know the rules, right?" She had a Russian accent.

"What rules?"

She rolled her eyes and leaned back in her chair.

"When are those pussies going to grow some balls and go over the fine print with you new guys?" She was obviously irritated.

"I signed the contracts. Is there a problem?"

"What Scott failed to tell you is that if I stamp that ticket, I'll give you your check for $100,000, but you can never see your daughter again."

"What do you mean?"

"Well, if we give you something of such magnitude, then you must give us something in return. As the contract states, we want your daughter. Once I stamp your ticket, I will give you a check for $100,000 and $100,000 for every ticket after that, but you will never see your daughter again."

I thought to myself that I wanted to use the money for my daughter so I would be able give her everything I couldn't afford before. I didn't care about myself; I cared about her!

"Screw you, lady, you can keep your money! What kind of a place is this?" I screamed.

"You would be surprised what men will give up for money." She started laughing at me.

"Well, you can keep it. I don't want anything to do with you or this company. I'd rather be poor."

"Okay, honey, it's your choice." She waved her hand for me to go away.

I ripped up the ticket and threw it at her. I walked into the warehouse and punched Scotty right in the face. He fell to the ground.

"What the hell, man?" His nose was broken.

"Fuck you! Stay away from me and my daughter. Do you hear me!"

He just nodded his head.

"If I see you again I'll finish you off for good!"

I grabbed the contracts off the desk and stormed out of the warehouse. When I got to my truck, I took a minute to read the fine print. It seems that they would sell their employees' kids to wealthy families all over the world as sex slaves. In exchange, whenever a salesman called them, they were obligated to buy certain stocks to drive a particular market up. That's how they made so much money. I looked down at my watch. I noticed it was time for my daughter to get out of school, and I had to pick her up. I started my truck and drove out of there. Linda was right. Some men will do terrible things for money, but not this guy.

Squirters

Throughout my years of sexual experiences with women, I have always been fascinated by what I call "squirters," or women who ejaculate when they come. I first experienced this at a young age and didn't have a clue what the fuck was going on. I don't think my girlfriend did either, but she said it felt INCREDIBLE! NO ONE had ever made her come like that! So from that moment on, I dedicated my life to mastering that art form. A never-ending search for every woman's G-spot!

Definition of a squirter:

All women have a functional prostate gland, about the size of their thumb, that surrounds their Urethra. Just like a male prostate, it produces fluid, beginning at puberty. Within the prostate gland there can be an area of increased sensitivity, more commonly referred to as the G-Spot. The G-Spot is located somewhere along the length of the Urethra. When the prostate gland is stimulated, many women experience female ejaculation, and a distinctive type of orgasm, a vaginal orgasm, one that is different from that experienced during clitoral stimulation alone. Some women cum, as in ejaculate, during sexual arousal, prior to orgasm, even without G-Spot stimulation. There is muscle tissue that surrounds the prostate gland that contracts during orgasm, potentially expelling its contents. There is some debate about the origin of *all* the fluid that is released during female ejaculation, as the prostate gland itself is relatively small, yet some women release up to two cups of liquid. Nevertheless, the liquid released during female ejaculation is not the same as urine. The best way to stimulate the G-Spot is through rhythmic massage with the fingers, a penis, or dildo. It may take practice to locate and connect with the G-Spot, and to learn how to experience vaginal orgasms that are accompanied by female ejaculation. G-Spot and vaginal orgasms aren't nearly as common as clitoral orgasms, some women always experience them, others never.

I wish to hell I knew this when I was a kid!

My first experience with this phenomenon was with my first real girlfriend, Liza. I mean "real" because she was the first girl I had sex with on a daily basis for about four years from when I was age sixteen to twenty. I had had sex with a few girls before her but nothing like with Liza. Somewhere in the middle there, maybe when we were about eighteen or so, I nailed it! The box spring of my bed was on the ground because I didn't have one of those metal racks with wheels underneath. I was on my knees facing the edge of the bed, and Liza was on her back with her ass on the edge of the bed and her legs up in the air. It was the perfect height. My cock must have been thrusting upward in the perfect way, and I hit her G-spot. She started moaning like I'd never heard her moan before.

"I'm coming. Oh god I'm coming. Jesus, Jack, what are you doing?"

"I don't know," I said confused, but totally into it.

"Ohhhhhhh god, fuck me! I'm coming," she screamed.

For the first time in my life, I felt like a porn star but had no clue what the hell I was doing. When she came, she squirted all over my cock and balls. At first I was grossed out because I didn't know what was happening.

"Don't stop, Jack! Harder, fuck me harder!"

She was grabbing my arms so hard her nails were digging into my skin. I kept pumping, and soon she came again. She squirted again, but this time not as much. When we finally finished, there was a big wet spot on the edge of my bed and on the rug between my knees. My knees had bloody rug burns on them. It was the middle of summer, so it was very hot, and we were both sweating profusely. We had fucked hundreds of times before, but I had never made her come twice and definitely NEVER made her squirt like that. My dad never told me about the "birds and the bees" or how to use a condom or how to shave and shit like that. I guess things like that embarrassed him, so I just winged it. I didn't even know that a woman squirting was possible. We had been drinking a lot that day, and I just chalked it up to that. Again, I was pretty young and actually thought it was kinda gross. I never made Liza cum like that again. She begged me to do it again, and believe me, I tried over the next few years we were together to no avail. Her G-spot eluded me like a thief in the night.

After Liza and I finally broke up for the last time of many times, you know how that shit goes with your high school sweetheart. I was with a few girls but not on a daily basis like her. One of the girls I met after Liza was Mimi. Mimi was a bartender at a bar called Fuzzy Bears that I went to on a daily basis. She had just started working there, and we hooked up almost immediately. Mimi was a few years older than me; I was only twenty-one, and she must have been twenty-seven, twenty-eight. Anyway, she swooped on me like a fuckin' stealth bomber. I had long hair down to my ass at the time; it was 1989, so it was still kinda cool, and she LOVED it. We had been going out for a while when I told her about Liza squirting that one time, but I could never get her to do it again. I'll never forget the smile Mimi gave me.

"I can show you how to do it to me."

"You can?" I was kinda surprised. I can honestly say that I learned a lot more from Mimi than my dad could have ever taught me!

"Sure, honey. After I get off work were gonna have some fun."

After her shift was done, I was pretty drunk. She would give me a free pitcher of beer for each one I paid for, and I could drink six to eight, sometimes ten pitchers by myself no problem depending on how long her shift was. She wouldn't even give me a mug; I'd just drink straight out of the side of the pitcher. That was my thing, and I was the only one in the bar who was allowed to do that. Everyone else had to use mugs. Even when I played pool, I'd take the whole pitcher over to the table. Anyway, when we got back to her apartment, my lessons began.

"Come here, baby," she said with that "I'm gonna teach you some shit, kid" smile.

I walked over to her bed, and she was laying down on it naked. Now remember I am REALLY drunk. I stood at the edge of her bed weaving back and forth.

"Lay down here next to me."

I laid down next to her.

"Take your middle finger and put it inside my pussy."

I put my finger inside her.

"Now feel around in there real softly."

I did it.

"Now I want you to make your finger like a hook." Take notes here, kids and or adults who still don't know what the fuck you're doing.

"Do you feel that soft bump that's on the backside of my clit?

I did.

"Take the tip of your finger and start banging me with your finger still in the shape of a hook and hit that spot."

I did what she told me, and she started moaning. It seemed to be working. I started doing it harder, and she started moaning louder just like Liza. After about a minute or two, she was squirming all over the bed. She took her middle finger and put it in her mouth and put some spit on it then she started rubbing her clit as I banged her.

"Don't stop! Keep going! I'm gonna come!" she screamed.

Right after she said that, she came and squirted all over my hand! Just like Liza had.

"You did great, baby," she said proudly.

"See, I told you I could teach you. Now if you can just bend me around into a position where your cock can hit that spot, I can squirt like that most of the time."

I just laid there for a minute. Now I know how the cavemen must have felt when they discovered the wheel. The first time Columbus saw the New World. The world wasn't flat; it was round like the moon. The first time Neil Armstrong set foot on the moon. Well, you get the picture. Anyway, she went on to say that she couldn't do it every time but if I did it right, most of the time, and she was right. Mimi was pretty small, about 5' 4", 115 pounds, with fake tits. I am 6' 2", 200 pounds, and no fake tits, so it was easy for me to grab her and twist her around into lots of different positions, and I got pretty good after a while. A few months later, she got her friend Kristy a job at Fuzzy Bears, and I was there the night she started. By this time, Mimi was my full-on girlfriend, so I hadn't tried my newfound skills on anyone else yet. Mimi had told Kristy what she had taught me and how good I had gotten. I guess you can see where this is going. We started getting buzzed, and before long, Kristy was all over me. Mimi was a lot smaller than us and got drunk pretty quick. She started talking about us all doing a threesome when they got off work. I learned another valuable lesson from Mimi that night. Nine times out of ten when you have a threesome with two girls, you're gonna lose them both. A guy cannot compete with the knowledge a woman has for another woman. Men are greedy by nature and will want to keep them both, but unless you have a lot of money or some other circumstance like that, you haven't got a chance. I didn't have a lot of money. After they got off work, we went to Mimi's apartment and partied and banged then banged some more. I showed Kristy my newfound skills, and she loved it! Then Mimi, then Kristy, then Mimi again. We took a smoke/beer break and then lathered, rinsed, repeated all night. In the morning, I felt like the king of the world. I woke up, and Kristy was all snuggled up next to me, but Mimi wasn't there. I got up and took a piss and then walked into the living room. Mimi was sitting on the couch smoking a cigarette, and I could tell by the look on her face that she was not happy. Long story short, she told me that she was pissed because I paid more attention to Kristy the night before than her. Translation: she was sober and realized that she had gotten drunk and let her best friend fuck her boyfriend, and now Kristy liked me, *a lot!* That was the beginning of the end. Mimi broke up with me, and she and Kristy started banging each other and she squeezed my talented young ass right out. She quit Fuzzy Bears, and that was the last I saw of my little Mimi.

Now Teri was a squirter from the get-go! The first time we had sex was in the front seat of her car. Her car had a sunroof, and she had a short skirt on that night. It was pretty late at night, and we were outside my house. I don't remember why we didn't just go inside, but I learned soon enough that it REALLY turned Teri on to have sex in public, something I didn't do too much of with Liza or Mimi. Mimi had given me a blow job on an Amtrak train coming back from Mexico one time, but that's about it. We were making out in her car, and I really didn't think I was gonna get lucky with her that night. I had already had sex with her younger sister Jenny a few times, which is how I met her, but she didn't know that at the time. They both figured that one out later. When we parked, I didn't sense that she wanted to go in the house, but she had already planned out how it was going to go down in her head unbeknownst to me.

"Let's do it," she said to me.

"Where?" I said.

"Here in my car."

"Why don't we go in the house?"

"Why don't we not?"

She took off her heels and pulled down her panties from under her skirt and threw them into the backseat. Then she hit the button, and her sunroof opened. She moved over to the passenger side of the car and climbed on top of me. It was kinda cramped and awkward, but after a few adjustments, we hit our stride. She was pretty tall for a chick, maybe about 5' 10", and her head and shoulder were sticking up through the sunroof as she pumped up and down. I had had Mimi in this position many times, so I did my thing. Teri EXPLODED! I mean she squirted all over my balls, the car seat, and the carpet on the floor of her car. It was a mess! I hadn't seen anything like that before. Three to four times more fluid than the other girls put together, maybe more. My pants were around my ankles, and they were all wet too. After she left, I went in my house and immediately took my pants and boxers off and put them in the washer. The next morning, Teri called me on the telephone and informed me that she and Jenny had had a very interesting conversation about me over breakfast and that they BOTH wanted to talk to me together. *Shit*, I thought, *I'm fucked!* Mimi and Kristy all over again. But wait. This time they were sisters, so obviously they weren't going to lezbo off with each other and dump me, at least I hoped not. They could, on the other hand, shoot me and dump me in a ditch somewhere. I was kinda nervous when I pulled up to their house and walked up to the door. Teri answered the door, and we walked into the kitchen. On the kitchen table was a beer waiting for me; it was cold. We sat down and Teri began.

"Jenny and I had a very interesting conversation about you this morning," she said very seriously.

"And?" I said.

"It seems you have been having sex with both of us, right?"

"Well, with you just once." I looked around the place real fast to see if anyone else was there to kill me.

"Well, it wouldn't be right for us both to date you. That would be pretty fucking sick! Wouldn't you agree?"

"Not necessarily, but continue."

"Well, we think it would be, so we've decided to let you choose."

"Choose what?"

"Me or Jenny."

"But I like both of you. Can I choose both?"

It was worth a shot. This was by far a weirder situation than with Mimi and Kristy. I was in uncharted waters here.

"You can't have us both. You have to choose."

"I can't. I like you both."

"We both like you too. That's why you have to choose one of us. You can't have both."

Jenny just sat there smiling quietly. What the hell was she thinking?

"So what do you think, Jen?"

"What she said." She pointed at Teri.

"Well, I met you first," I said.

"Then you banged my sister." She had a point.

"Can I think about it?"

"No. You have to tell us now!" Jenny said sounding a little pissed off.

I took a drink from my beer and started to think. This was NOT the scenario I had expected when I was driving over here at all. I decided to do pros and cons.

I had met Jenny first. She was very pretty, but kind of a tomboy, hippyish. She was small with long straight light-brown hair but dressed in denim overalls a lot. She liked the same movies and music as I did but was only 19 (I was 22) and couldn't get into bars most of the time. She wasn't very good in bed either, probably because of her age, and didn't have a job.

Teri, on the other hand, was beautiful, and Jenny knew it. Teri was the older sister, 21, so she was only one year younger than me. She could get into bars and was the leader of the two. She was tall with the same length of hair as Jenny's but a little darker brown. Beautiful eyes, light-brown eyes, and a gorgeous smile. She dressed a lot better and sexier than her sister, but this is probably because she had a really good job. She also had a very nice car with a sunroof. The only thing that concerned me was how she sprang a leak like a goddamn oil tanker when she came the night before. Her pros outweighed her cons by far.

Verdict: Teri.

"I'm sorry Jenny, after last night, I have to go with Teri. No hard feelings, babe. I still care about you a lot and would kill anybody who fucks with you."

Teri got up excitedly.

"I knew you would pick me! I just knew it! Oh I love you."

As far as women go, this was truly the strangest experience I had had in my young life. After this I learned that I should never try to predict what a woman would say or do. EVER! They are mysteries that only God knows because he molded them from man's ribs, and we weren't ever getting that fucker back. I had a newfound respect for women and what they were capable of. Cheers, girls.

Teri and I dated off and on for many years. I never had sex with her sister again. She and Jenny moved from Orange County to Los Angeles because her job moved her there. I devised a way to put a hefty trash bag down over her bed so that her cum gushers wouldn't soak the bed so bad we couldn't sleep in it. I got used to her squirting orgasms and didn't think it was gross anymore. I actually started to like it! I got quite creative and used to get scissors and cut the trash bags into different sizes to fit different locations. We even took bags to Vegas a few times. We could also put a bag on the floor and do it doggy-style to not soak the carpet. We found the shower to be quite practical as well. No cleanup required in there. Sometimes, Jenny would come home at night, and our trash bags would be on the floor because we'd pass out and not throw them away, and she'd get mad. One time, we came home and we were all hot and horny, and I was too lazy to get a bag (that was my job), so I got an ingenious idea! We did it in Jenny's bed (they ALWAYS shared a room no matter how many rooms were in the house they lived in, and there were a few of them). Jenny came home with her boyfriend and was pissed!

They went and slept on the couch that night. Classic. Teri was the first girlfriend that I had that was my bro. We would drink and write poetry together all night. I would play guitar, and we would write songs together too. She was my lover and my best friend. She even tried to teach me how to speak French (she was fluent in French), but my brain couldn't handle it. She would get mad at me and cuss me out in French, and it would turn me on so bad I thought my head would explode, which of course made her even madder. I would ask Jenny to translate what she said for me, and she would just say, "You don't want to know." She was also the first person to take me to an actual gym to work out. I used to just lift weights in my garage to work out and had never even been on a treadmill before. I still go to the gym to work out to this day because of her. Probably one of the only "positive" things I've done for my body in my life, and I'm probably still alive and in halfway decent shape because of it. Teri was the closest thing I ever got to a soul mate in my life till now (I am forty-nine as I write this). We were on one of our "breakups" when I met another girl at the Roxy in Hollywood. We had only been dating for a few months, and she got pregnant. I was still talking to Teri and told her what had happened. I told her that we were going to keep it, and I was going to do the right thing and try and make it work with the mom. She was bummed but understood and still wanted to be friends. Awesome chick! Well, things didn't work out with the mom, and I was back with Teri before the kid was even born. My daughter was born on July 25, 1993. Teri and Jenny loved that child! Especially Teri. They bought her little outfits and toys and even kept baby stuff to change into and play with at their house for when we came over. They even started calling each other her aunties and were going to teach her how to speak French. One day, she told me that she got a promotion at work and was very excited. The company told her if she wanted it she had to move to New York, though, or she could stay in California and pass up the opportunity; it was up to her. At first, she wanted me to move to New York with her. I couldn't, of course, because my daughter wasn't even a year old at that time, and I couldn't leave her. I decided at that moment that I loved her so much that I had to break up with her. For real this time. I knew if I didn't, she would stay in L.A. to be with me and miss this opportunity of a lifetime. I know when opportunity knocks, you have to open that door quick, or it can pass you by, and I wasn't about to let her pass it up just to stay with my sorry ass. So I broke up with her. At first, she thought it was just like all the other times and we'd get back together, but I stood my ground. It was probably one of the hardest things I've ever done in my life. I really did love and care for that girl immensely. It was Christmastime, but I wouldn't take her calls. Jenny called one time, and I talked to her.

"What are you doing, Jack? Why won't you talk to Teri? She is devastated. She won't even eat. She loves you so much. I love you too. You're like my big brother. I never had a brother. You've always looked out for us over the years. Why are you doing this to her?" she asked almost crying.

"Tell her that I don't love her anymore, and I don't ever want to speak to her again. Good-bye, baby girl." I hung up the phone, sat there on my bed, and started to cry. That did it for sure. I would never talk to Teri or Jenny again. That weekend, Teri drove down to Orange County all the way from Los Angeles. She knocked on the door, left a Christmas present on my porch, then ran back to her car and drove away. When I opened the door, there was the present on the ground, and I briefly saw the back end of her car as it went around the corner. That was the last time I saw her, or at least her car. I reached down and picked up the present. The tag read: "Merry Christmas. Love, Auntie Teri and Auntie Jenny." I opened it, and there was a beautiful little tan dress with white stockings and a bow for her hair. It obviously looked very expensive. My guess is she bought it somewhere in Beverly Hills. She must have moved to New York because I never heard from her again. To this day, I don't think she knows why I did what I did. It was one of the most unselfish things I've ever done in my life. She's a very smart girl, so I like to think that she does know why and forgives me for it, but I guess I'll never know. I still miss her a lot. Even my friends still talk about her. I really did love that chick. Teri was the queen of the squirters! I have never seen another woman squirt orgasms like that, and I don't think I ever will.

US Festival '83

It was early 1983 when I heard them announce it on the radio. The computer millionaire Steve Wozniak was going to finance another three-day US Festival in San Bernardino, California. I was only fourteen years old at the time. I didn't go to the festival the year before, but the bands playing in '83 were some of my favorites! They announced that on day number two the lineup of bands would be Motley Crue, Joe Walsh, Ozzy Osbourne, Judas Priest, Triumph, Scorpions, and closing the concert would be Van Halen. I had to go! So I needed a plan.

I called all my friends, and none of their parents would let them go. Fuck! Now that I think about it, we were only fourteen years old, and there was going to be thousands of people there, so frankly I think a lot of my friends were afraid to go. Not me, though! I had seen bands at some local club shows and a few arena concerts but nothing of this size or magnitude. I had *no idea* what I was getting myself into. My fifteenth birthday was coming up in April. The festival was at the end of May. Maybe I could talk my parents into getting me a ticket for my birthday. I knew that my dad wouldn't give a shit. All he would care about was how much the ticket was. They were only twenty bucks, so that was an easy sell. My mom, on the other hand, was the hard sell. She would want to know how I was going to get there, who I was going to be with, how much money would I need, all that kind of stuff. I had to prepare my case using poise and strategy. Basically, I was going to lie my ass off! I heard about a thing called the "US BUS" that would drive you to the festival and back home for $15. Okay, now I was up to thirty-five bucks. I would also need money for pot and a T-shirt. This was going to be more expensive than I thought! That night when we all sat down to eat dinner would be my opportunity to sell my pitch. I cleaned up my room and did my homework early to get prepared. When my dad got home from work, I sat in the living room and started talking to him about the LA Dodgers. He loved the Dodgers; we talked all the way up till it was dinnertime. Then I switched it on for my mom by getting all the plates and silverware out for her. It was perfect. When we sat down to eat, I patiently waited for a break in the conversation to start my plan.

"I want to go to a concert for my birthday this year," I calmly told my mother.

"Oh really, what band do you want to go see?"

"It's actually a festival, and there are going to be a bunch of cool bands there. All my favorites. It's going to be awesome!" I tried not to oversell it, but I was genuinely excited!

"A bunch of bands? How much is this going to cost me?" my dad chimed in.

"It's only twenty bucks for seven bands, Dad, that's only like $3 a band. Totally cheap. What a bargain, huh!" I knew if I broke it down like that, he'd go for it.

"Where is it at?"

"Glen Helen Park. Please, all my friends are going. It's going to be so much fun!" I tried to deflect any more questions about the bus. My younger brother looked at me like he knew I was full of shit but said nothing.

"Who else is going?" my mom said. My dad was out of the picture now.

"Well, let's see. Brian is going, and Robert, Mike, Jimmy, all those guys." I was lying through my teeth now, but I had to keep my cool.

"And their parents said it was okay?"

"Oh yeah. We just all need to get our tickets and then we're gonna meet up there." I knew I would be alone.

"I just need to get my ticket as soon as possible before it sells out!" There was no way in hell that this concert was going to sell out, but I had to emphasize the urgency of the matter.

"Well, your father and I will have to discuss it, and we'll let you know." The first phase of my plan was complete, and it went off without a hitch. Now I just had to sell my mom on the bus ride, and I was in!

When I got home from school, I planned on asking my mom if she had talked to my dad about me going to the festival. My mom was always good about convincing my dad to let me do things that he normally wouldn't let me do. Like letting a fifteen-year-old kid go alone to a festival where approximately one hundred thousand people would be attending. She knew it meant a lot to me, though, so she worked her magic. After all, it was the biggest event of the year.

"So did you talk to Dad? Can I go?" I asked eagerly.

"Yes, I did, and of course he said no."

"But all my friends are going! I'm going to be the only one who doesn't go!" I was lying. None of my friends' parents would let them go.

"Well, I know this means a lot to you, so I convinced your father to let you go. Just don't make me regret this, Jack."

"I promise you I won't get into any trouble."

"Okay, I just don't want to have to tell your father that we need to drive all the way out to San Bernardino to get you."

"No problem! I'll just get a ticket for the US Bus. They'll give me and my friends a ride to the festival and a ride back home. All you have to do is drop me off at Fullerton College."

"They have a bus. Well, let's go get your tickets before your father gets home from work and changes his mind."

My mom and I got in her car (I was still too young to drive) and drove to the Music Plus record store. I bought my US Bus ticket for $15 and a US Festival ticket for $20. Can you believe that? I spend more than that on beer at concerts now. The festival was to be held on May 28. I couldn't wait!

The morning of the festival, I got up very early. We had to be at the college by 6:00 a.m. for me to catch the bus. It was still dark outside as I got my things together. I had a cheap old camera from when I was a boy in the '70s, but it didn't have a strap to go around my wrist. That had broken off long ago. It was too big to fit in my pocket, so I had to find something to replace the strap, otherwise I would have to carry it around all day. The only thing I could find was some kite string. I tripled up the string and put it through the loop. I made it long enough to go over my head and around my neck. Basically I made a camera necklace. It would have to do. When we got to the college, I had to figure out a way to get away from my mom so she wouldn't figure out that I was going to be alone. I spotted a group of kids that looked about my age.

"There's some of my friends right there! You can just drop me off here."

"I don't recognize any of those kids." Her mother senses knew something wasn't right.

"They're kids from school. You don't know them."

"Well, where are your other friends?"

"They must be around here somewhere. I'll find them when we get on the bus."

Reluctantly she stopped the car and I got out.

"Be careful out there! I love you."

"Okay, I love you too. I'll see you back here tonight."

I walked over to the group of kids and pretended to know them. Once my mom had driven away, I went over to the bus and lit up a cigarette. Now I was on my own.

The bus driver announced that he would be letting everybody on the bus and to have your boarding passes ready. I was one of the first in line, so I took a seat near the back of the bus. In the seat behind me was a hippie couple. They looked to be in their early twenties. The man tapped me on the shoulder.

"Hey there, kid. Are you all alone?" he said.

"Yeah. None of my friends' parents would let them go so I came by myself."

"How old are you?"

"Fifteen."

"You've got a lot of balls! Do you know how many people are going to be out there today?" the woman asked.

"About one hundred thousand?" I guessed.

"Try tripling that!" she said.

The biggest crowd I had seen at that point in my life was a concert at the Long Beach Sports Arena. That place only holds about thirteen thousand people. I had no idea what I was about to see when I got off that bus!

"My name is Morpheus, and she is Star," he announced.

"We brought a bunch of drugs to sell at the festival. Have you ever take acid before?"

"Yeah, I've done it a few times," I said confidently. I know it's not a good thing, but I really had done acid more than a few times by the time I was fifteen.

"Well, we have two different kinds today. This one is Blue Unicorn, and this one is Red Star. I named that one after my girlfriend." Star had red hair.

"Let's all do one together, Morpheus!" Star said excitedly.

"Okay, kid, which one do you want?"

"I guess I'll have to go with the Red Star."

"One Red Star coming up."

Star clapped her hands and then made "peace" signs with her fingers. Morpheus told me to stick out my tongue. He placed the paper blotter on it and then did the same with Star. Finally he dosed himself. The sun was coming up on the horizon, and I thought to myself that this was going to a very interesting day. We made small talk as the bus drove down the freeway. They said they were from Venice Beach and owned a little head shop there on the boardwalk. Star was sitting next to the window. She reached up and slid it down. Morpheus got a joint out of his cigarette pack and lit it up. He handed it to me and I took a hit. We passed it around to a few of the other people sitting around us. The bus driver didn't say shit. Apparently, the US Bus was a drug-friendly vehicle. As we approached Glen Helen Regional Park, I really didn't feel the acid.

"Hey, Morpheus, I don't feel this acid coming on."

"Give it time, kid, believe me, you'll feel it."

"Why don't you let me try one of those Blue Unicorns?"

"Wow! You really do have big balls." Star was impressed.

"Well, you know the rules, kid, the first one's free." Morpheus put out the palm of his hand.

"How much?" I asked.

"For you, two bucks."

I gave him $2, and we went through the tongue ritual again. I told them that I was going to take a piss, and I ditched them. They would just slow me down. I had plans on getting up to the front of the crowd for the first band. I never saw them again. Now that I think back, I wonder if they are still together. Or even still alive. They would most likely be in their late fifties today. I know most hippies mate for life, so I'd like to think that they still have that little shop in Venice. I made my way through the crowd and parked cars up to the front gate.

When I got to the gate, there was a very large crowd of people in front of it. Security guards where standing on the other side keeping people from sneaking in. They would be opening the gates at 8:00 a.m., and the bands would start performing at noon. It was 7:45 a.m. I tried to squeeze my way up to the front. The head security guard announced in a very loud voice that when they opened the gates, he wanted everyone to walk into the park in a calm and orderly fashion. Of course, the exact opposite happened. When the gates were opened, BASH, everyone started running! I was near the front of the pack, so I was all right, but some of the slower people that were in the middle of the crowd fell and got trampled over. It was survival of the fittest! I ran into this huge open space of land. It must have been a couple of miles wide. My heart was pounding from the rush of the gate race, and now I definitely felt the acid coming on! I looked to my right and saw this huge stage, scaffolding with lights, and at the top was a big sign that said "US '83." I went over and leaned right on the plywood barrier and snapped a few pictures of the stage and the sign. People were laying out blankets and food. Some started drinking alcohol, beer, and smoking joints. I didn't know it at the time, but those spots would be filled with thousands of people in just a few short hours. I stayed in my spot against the plywood all the way till noon. The first band that was scheduled to play was Quiet Riot. For some reason, they had taken the place of Joe Walsh on the schedule. I was familiar with them because Randy Rhoads was in their band before Ozzy stole him, and then he died in a plane crash a year earlier. When

Quiet Riot finally came on and Carlos Cavazo hit that first guitar note, people started rushing the stage. All those people sitting on blankets got trampled over. Not only did they lose their spots, but most of the stuff they had laying on the ground got trampled too. I was pushed up against the plywood with great force. After a few songs, the pushing forward eased up a bit, and I caught a breather. Quiet Riot played a great set and got the crowd going. I snapped three pictures of them. It was a good start to the day.

Motley Crue was the next band to play. I wish I could say the same kind things about them as I did for Quiet Riot, but I can't. They sucked! I don't know if they were drunk, or on drugs, or had technical difficulties or what. They just didn't sound good to me. I clicked one picture of them and then decided I would leave my spot in the front and go get something to eat. I elbowed my way through the crowd toward the concession stands. When I got through the initial people watching the band and out into the open, I realized just how big this festival really was. I was frying on acid, and it literally blew my mind! I was fifteen years old in a sea of four hundred thousand people, and I didn't know any of them. There was a main dirt "road" going through the middle of the crowd. The people up here had little campsites and sleeping bags and blankets laid out. You could hear the music good from up there, and there was the biggest TV monitor I had ever seen showing the band play. Motley Crue didn't sound any better from up there either. As I traveled up the road, I saw a large Indian teepee. It had hundreds of men's ties on the ground outside, and they went all the way around it. I asked one of the guys standing by it what was going on, and he told me if you put a quarter in the slot, the man inside would play you a song, and then you could have a tie. I was starting to peak on the two hits of acid I took, so this sounded very interesting to me! I got a quarter out of my pocket and put it through the slot. The man inside started playing "Row, Row, Row Your Boat" on a kazoo. I was tripping out. Was this really happening? After he was finished with the song, he said, "Now you may choose a tie, my son." I bent down and picked a tie from the pile on the ground and tied it around my head like a bandana. After that very odd experience, I went over to the concession stand and bought a hot dog and a coke. I found some shade under a tree and sat down. After I ate, I saw a booth with a girl who was selling programs. I went over and bought one. There was a schedule of bands and set times in the program. Ozzy Osbourne was going to be the next band on stage. Ozzy was the band that I most wanted to see not only because he is my favorite singer, but also his guitarist Randy Rhoads had died a year earlier, and I was curious to hear his new guitarist Jake E. Lee play live. I started to make my way back down the dirt road, and as I did, I passed by a man holding a sign that said "FREE ACID." I thought, *What the hell, one more won't hurt*, and walked over to him and stuck my tongue out. He put a tab on my tongue, and I swallowed it. When I got down to the crowd, I elbowed my way up as far as I could. It was very hot and sweaty down near the front. I realized very quickly that it would be impossible for me to get to my old spot against the plywood. People were passing out from heat exhaustion and being passed over the front rails where security would take them to the medical tent. There were men on platforms with water cannons spraying the crowd. I remember thinks how good it felt when they sprayed me with one. The guy that organized and paid for the festival, Steve Wozniak, came on stage and asked everyone to please take one step back. That did not happen. Finally, after what seemed forever, Ozzy came on stage. He was wearing some kind of brown leather witch doctor outfit complete with a big headdress with long feathers sticking out of the top. As the band started their first song, he ripped off his shirt and threw it in the crowd. Everyone went apeshit! Jake E. Lee played the Randy Rhoads songs and guitar solos great, which is no easy task. I took some more pictures of Ozzy. The band sounded awesome! Judas Priest was up next. They always put on a great live show. Especially in 1983. They had just finished a world tour, and the band was tight! To this day, it is the only time I've ever seen them play during the daytime. After Judas Priest, the band Triumph was scheduled. I wasn't very familiar with them. I knew they were from Canada and had heard a few of their songs on the radio, so I decided to take a break and watch them on the monitors. I was very thirsty, so I went over to the beer gardens. Of course, I wasn't twenty-one so I couldn't get in, but that never stopped me before. I went around the side to see if I could sneak in and I found a small hole in the chain-link fence. I squeezed my body through, and I was in. I didn't have a twenty-one-or-over wristband, so I would have get someone to buy me a beer. I found a guy that looked pretty drunk and asked him to buy me a beer. I gave him the last bit of money that I had, and he got me a big ice-cold beer. It tasted so good going down. I finished up the beer and went back out into the festival. It was still hot out, but the beer helped me cool down. The third hit of acid was going strong, so I sat next to these people who had one of those little camps. They were a married couple and told me they had a son who was about my age. The woman gave me a sandwich to eat and some water. How cool was it that total strangers gave me food and water. It was like everyone at the festival was part of a huge family. I didn't see anyone being negative or fighting. Just peace and happiness through music all around. I thanked them for their kindness and headed toward the T-shirt booth. The food helped, but I was still frying pretty good. I waited in line, and when I got to the front, I ordered the coolest shirt they had. The guy brought it over, but when I reached in my pocket, I didn't have any money. I had forgotten that I spent it all in the beer gardens. I was devastated! The one thing that I wanted the most I couldn't get. I told the guy that I had lost all my money and I couldn't buy the shirt. I turned and started walking away. I don't know if it was the look on my face or if he just felt sorry for me, but he yelled, "Hey, kid." When I turned around to see what he wanted, he threw me the shirt for free. I couldn't believe it! I couldn't believe how generous and cool everyone I met there was! Triumph would be the last band to play during the daytime. The Scorpions and Van Halen would be playing under that massive scaffolding of lights.

I caught a second wind with my little rest while Triumph played and started back down to the stage for the Scorpions. The sun had set, and it was dark out now. Surprisingly I made it pretty close to the front. I checked my camera, and I only had one picture left. I would save that last photo for Van Halen. The Scorpions came on stage and put on a great show. If you've ever seen them before, they have A LOT of energy! Their light show was incredible. I would have to say that they stole the show. In my opinion, the Scorpions were the best band of the day. The encore song was basically them jumping around and rolling on the stage with their mouths wide open for ten minute. Then it was over. Van Halen, on the other hand, had been having a huge party backstage all day long. In between bands, David Lee Roth would come up on the monitors dressed like Napoleon with girls in bikinis hanging all over him and say some random shit that didn't even make sense. It was obvious that he was wasted. It took a LONG time for Van Halen to come out on stage. I would say over an hour at least. When they did finally come out, they were all completely smashed. The bass player Michael Anthony was drinking a fifth of Jack Daniels right out of the bottle. Eddie Van Halen was just stumbling around with a big-ass smile but somehow still playing amazing guitar. Some guy in the front row threw something on stage, and it almost hit David Lee Roth, so he found the guy in the crowd who threw it and threatened to take his girlfriend backstage and fuck her. The crowd loved that! After all, they were the mighty Van Halen, so they could pull that kind of shit off, unlike Motley Crue earlier that day. In 1983, Van Halen was one of the biggest bands in the world. Steve Wozniak paid them $1 million to headline the US Festival. That was an insane amount of money at that time. I don't know how, but they put on a really good concert that night! After Van Halen, that was it. The festival was over. Everyone looked exhausted. I know that I was. I made my way up the hill and into the parking lot. It took me a while, but I finally found my bus. I got on the bus, found a seat, and passed out.

I woke up to this buzzing alarm sound. I looked up, and the bus was stopped. The driver was standing over me looking at me with a frown on his face. My left arm was on the handle of the emergency exit door on the side of the bus. When I was sleeping, I accidentally leaned on it causing the alarm to go off. The driver moved me over to another seat and then leaned over and fixed the door. The alarm went off. It had woken up everybody on the bus, and they were all staring at me. At least I felt like they were. I just closed my eyes and went back to sleep. I had no idea what time it was when we got back to the college parking lot. I got off the bus, and incredibly enough, I still had my camera, festival program, and T-shirt. It was good to see my mom waiting in her car. I walked over and got in. I slept all the next day into the early evening. I woke up at dinner then went back to bed. I had school the next day. Monday morning, I proudly wore my US Festival T-shirt to school. Only a handful of kids were wearing one, mostly seniors; I was the only freshman. I told all my friends what an amazing day it was and how they had missed out. I wasn't lying either. That was one of the best days of my life, and I spent it totally alone. Well, that is if you don't count the four hundred thousand anonymous strangers I shared the day with. I will never forget US Festival '83.